Catch a Falling Star

Catch a Falling Star

MEG McKINLAY

WALKER BOOKS
AND SUBSIDIARIES

LONDON • BOSTON • SYDNEY • AUCKLAND

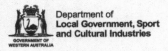
Department of
**Local Government, Sport
and Cultural Industries**
GOVERNMENT OF
WESTERN AUSTRALIA

This project is supported by the State Government through the
Department of Local Government, Sport and Cultural Industries.

First published in 2019
by Walker Books Australia Pty Ltd
Locked Bag 22, Newtown
NSW 2042 Australia
www.walkerbooks.com.au

A catalogue record for this
book is available from the
NATIONAL
LIBRARY National Library of Australia
OF AUSTRALIA

ISBN: 978 1 925381 20 7

COVER IMAGES: (sky) Regine Heintz © Arcangel Images;
(trees) © Nutpacha Homthanathip/Shutterstock.com;
(stars) © rungrote/Shutterstock.com

Typeset in Perpetua
Printed and bound in Australia by McPherson's Printing Group

10 9

FSC
www.fsc.org
MIX
Paper from
responsible sources
FSC® C009448

The paper this book is printed on is certified against the
Forest Stewardship Council® Standards. Griffin Press holds
FSC chain of custody certification SGS-COC-005088. FSC
promotes environmentally responsible, socially beneficial
and economically viable management of the world's forests.

For my father,
who gave me both logic and magic, in equal measure.
There would be no stories without you.

One

It's 2.53 on a Friday when I find out the sky is falling.

At least I think that's what Jeremy Ricardo said. The sound is a bit muffled because of the plastic salad bowl on his head.

Jeremy's wearing the bowl and a puffy jacket because it's the closest he can get to a spacesuit. And he needs a spacesuit because he's going to be an astronaut when he grows up, just like Damien last week, and Trevor the time before. I don't know what the odds are of three kids from the same class in a tiny little town on the south coast of nowhere, Western Australia, becoming astronauts, but it seems like they'd be ... astronomical.

Ha. I look down at the desk so Mrs Easton won't see me smile, so she won't say, *What's so funny, Frankie?* and *Perhaps you could share it with the rest of the class?*

This isn't a rest-of-the-class joke. I'll save it for later, to tell my brother Newt. He might be only seven but he's obsessed with science of all kinds. He's even named after a scientist – Isaac Newton – which is how he got his nickname. He's probably got a better shot at being an astro-anything than Jeremy ever will.

"Interesting." Mrs Easton nods encouragingly. "Keep going."

She calls this "Fantastic Futures". She says because we're in Year Six now – almost high school! Almost kind-of-sort-of on our way to being grown up! – it's important we start thinking about what comes next. So when we have time last thing Friday, she chooses a couple of kids to give a little speech. It's the absolute simplest thing in the world, she says. All we have to do is talk *clearly and confidently* about what we want to do when we grow up, giving two *thoughtful and relevant* reasons for our choice.

So far today we've had Jenny King (*a teacher, because it's the best job in the world and because I want to be just like you, Mrs Easton*) and Darren Mackie (*a mechanic, because I like cars and because cars are unreal*).

And now Jeremy.

Kat slides a note across the double desk we share. In her neat, loopy handwriting, it reads:

Because space is amazing! And I also enjoy lettuce.

I stare straight ahead, biting my lip to stop myself laughing. Suddenly all I can see is Jeremy up in space taking his helmet off to toss himself a quick salad.

"It was in the newspaper," he says. "It probably won't hit anyone, but still."

This is my first clue that I may have misheard. I mean, if the sky's coming down, I'm pretty sure it's going to hit someone. I lean towards Kat. "What did he—?"

"Frankie Avery!" Mrs Easton's eyes narrow. "I hope you're listening?"

"I was," I say quickly. "I mean … I am."

"Excellent." She walks towards us between the rows of desks. "Then you'll be able to tell me what Jeremy said."

Kat's mouthing something I can't make out. She points towards the ceiling and mimes something dropping, going *splat!* on the desk.

Jeremy's muffled voice floats through my head and no matter how I twist it, it sounds the same. I know it can't be right but Mrs Easton's next to me now. She peers at me with her beady bird eyes and it's all I've got so I open my mouth and say it because what have I got to lose?

"Um … the sky's falling?"

Kat puts her head down on the desk. Laughter ripples around the room. Behind me, Marcus Simmonds crows, "Oh, no, Chicken Little. We must go and tell the king!"

Jeremy snorts. "Not *the* sky. Sky*lab*. It's a massive satellite or something. It was supposed to stay up in space but there was some kind of problem. The newspaper said something about a solar panel or ..."

There's more but I don't hear it. And it's not because of the salad bowl. It's because there's a roaring in my ears, drowning out everything else.

Because *Skylab*? It's a thing I know, a word I know. And when I hear it I'm back in the Space Shack on a chilly autumn night.

May 1973. Almost exactly six years ago. How many days? I would have known that once. I would have been counting.

I stopped all that in the end. I had to. Mum said we needed to let things go.

I thought I had. I thought I did. But suddenly it's right here. Suddenly Dad is right here, just like he was that last night.

He's wrapped a blanket around me and cranked back the panel in the roof. Above, the sky is bright with stars. Newt has more blankets on because he's only two and Mum doesn't like him being out in the cold.

"He's too little," she says. "He doesn't even know what he's looking at." But she lets Dad take him. Because it's Newt's birthday and even though he's already had his cake and his presents, Dad wants him to have one more thing.

10

He sits Newt on the stool next to the telescope and holds him while Mum snaps a photo.

Then we look up.

Not into the telescope tonight but through the open roof. It's better like this, Dad says, because the thing we're about to see is moving fast.

Dad puts Newt on his shoulders and I stand on my tippy-toes, as high as I can get. We stand on the telescope platform together, our faces turned to the clear night sky. And then we see it — a bright flash streaking overhead, blazing through the dark.

I tug on Dad's jacket. "Is it a shooting star?"

He smiles and shakes his head. "It's Skylab. One of the world's very first space stations. And a space station, my lovely Frankie, my lovely Newt, is nothing at all like a star."

He was right too. For one thing, stars don't fall to Earth. At least not this quickly — not after five years or even six. Stars are sure and steady; it takes millions and billions of years before their light even starts to fade. Stars are pretty much as forever as it gets.

But space stations are made by people. People who roll out metal and hammer in rivets and put it all together like Lego. People who do maths and make plans and blast things off into space and hope they got it right.

Skylab. It went up. It's coming down.

"They reckon it'll be next month. Or maybe July. Anyway ..."

Jeremy sucks in a deep breath and I lean forwards. There's something weird about him. Weirder than usual, I mean. The salad bowl's fogged up and he's swaying on his feet.

Despite the fact that this class apparently has one future nurse and two future doctors, none of us moves.

Mrs Easton lunges for Jeremy. She pulls the bowl off his head and sits him down.

"Deep breaths," she says. "Deep breaths."

Without meaning to, I do it too. The room becomes steadier. My mind clears.

After a minute Jeremy gets to his feet. He puts the salad bowl under his arm like he's just returned from a deep space mission to Mars. "So the reasons I want to be an astronaut are that I think space is really cool and if I work at NASA I can make sure stuff like this doesn't happen."

"Well done, Jeremy." Mrs Easton gives him a pat on the shoulder. "Maybe don't *wear* the bowl next time, though. When speaking in public, it's generally best not to faint from lack of oxygen."

She leads the class in a round of applause. I should clap too but I can't get my hands to move. All I can think about is Skylab up there, circling, falling.

And while Jeremy strides back to his seat, I wonder what it would be like to be someone who thinks you actually have control over things.

Who believes that if you want to, you can keep them from crashing to the ground.

Things That Fall
From the Sky

Lots of things. Normal things. Everyday things.

No one's surprised when a raindrop hits their windscreen, when a leaf lands at their feet.

Other things fall, too. Stranger things. Fish and frogs. Showers of them, like something in a story.

It was Kat who told me about that. It was in a book her mum got from *Reader's Digest* called *Strange Stories, Amazing Facts*. I sat next to her on their couch as she flicked through, reading out all this weird stuff. On one page, there was a drawing of people running for cover as fish rained on their heads. The book said some people thought it was the end of the world, that God's judgement had come upon them.

Newt laughed when Kat read that bit. He was sitting at the dining table, taking a transistor radio apart. We hadn't even known he was listening.

He set us straight about the fish and frogs. It doesn't mean the end of the world, he said. It's actually completely logical. Most things are when you really think about them.

And if you think it's strange that a seven-year-old is

explaining things to us, that's because you haven't met Newt. He's one of those kids who reads and watches and listens — books of interesting facts, *The Curiosity Show* on TV, science programs on the radio. And the next thing you know, he's telling you all about stuff. You're saying, *Isn't it weird how* ... and he gets this look on his face and his eyes flicker like he's looking something up in the filing cabinet in his brain, and he says, *Well, actually that's because* ... and *Did you know that, Frankie?*

The fish and frogs?

Actually, that's because of tornadoes. They scoop them up from rivers and lakes and the ocean. They suck them high into the air and whirl them around and around for hundreds of miles. Then they drop them somewhere completely unexpected, making people go *ooh* and *aah* and come up with wild and crazy theories.

Did you know that, Frankie?

I did not.

I can't imagine what it would be like to have frogs suddenly raining on your head. Or to be a frog, raining on someone. I can't think too much about those frogs — one minute minding their business in a pond, the next minute scooped up and flying through the air.

Maybe the flying part would make the landing worth it.

That's what I hope. That's what I try to believe.

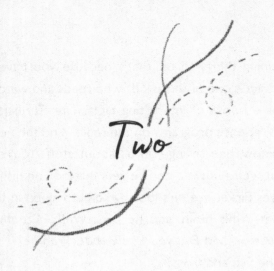

Two

"Are you okay?" Kat slides into the seat next to me. "You look kind of weird."

"Wow, thanks."

"You know what I mean."

We're on the bus after school. Revhead Ronnie's drumming his fingers on the steering wheel, the high school kids are throwing orange peel up the back and Newt's down the front with his nose in a comic. Outside, Dale's doing circles on his Malvern Star, getting ready to race us to the corner.

It's the same as always, only different. Inside my head, my thoughts are spinning like a wheel.

Ronnie jabs the door button and the bus lurches away from the kerb. By the time we reach the corner, Dale's a small dot behind us and Jeremy's hanging out the window blowing raspberries. As we head out of town, I lean forwards and grip the seat in front. Ronnie always takes the last bend too fast. It's like he can't wait to get out onto the highway, to plant his foot and cruise.

Kat frowns. "If you're feeling sick, you can come to my place."

It'd be easy to do that. Our house is half an hour away but Kat's is only five minutes, the very first stop. And until last year, when Mum decided we were old enough to be home alone, Newt and I used to go there all the time.

I'm not sick, though. I just feel strange. It's as if hearing that single word – *Skylab* – has opened a door, one I closed tightly a long time ago.

I suppose that's what's making me look *kind of weird*, but I can't tell Kat that. Instead, I force a smile. "I'm okay."

Even if I knew how to explain – about the weird tangle of Dad and Skylab, about how the night Skylab launched was the last night I saw him, about how all this stuff is suddenly right there making me feel wobbly and strange ... even if I could do that, I wouldn't. Because it's easier not to talk about Dad, even to Kat. Because whenever anyone mentions him, people get this look on their face. All of a sudden I stop being Frankie and turn into *that poor girl whose father died*.

"I've got stuff to do anyway." I nod towards the front of the bus. "You know."

"Oh, yeah. The birthday boy." Kat glances at the back of Newt's fair head. "I just don't get why you have to do it all."

"I don't *have* to," I say. "I want to."

It's mostly true.

Kat shrugs. Then she bumps me playfully with her shoulder. "Hey, how funny was Jeremy? Another astronaut. Sure thing."

"Yeah."

"Have you worked yours out yet?"

"Um ... not quite."

Kat sighs and I feel like doing the same. It's not as though I haven't tried; it just feels impossible. I can't imagine what I'm going to be doing next year, let alone for the rest of my life. How can it be nearly high school already? How can it be almost *1980*? The years are meant to start with seven, not eight. Eight sounds like the future, like science fiction, like ...

"Earth to Frankie!" Kat waves her hand in front of my face. "You'd better think of something soon."

"I know," I say. "Don't worry."

The tatty vinyl squeaks as she shifts in her seat. "I can help you next weekend if you want."

She's talking about Friday. I'm sleeping over at her

place so we can go and see *Superman* at the drive-in.

And I feel a bit guilty because the truth is I could do my Fantastic Futures talk easily if I pretended I was little again, back when I had everything worked out. When I was four and five and almost six and Dad and I used to spend every spare minute in the Space Shack and there was only one thing I could possibly be when I grew up and that was an astronomer – not for a hobby like Dad but an official real one who would probably one day discover a new planet.

I've never told Kat that, even though she's my best friend. Because that was *before* and this is *after*.

I nod. "Yeah, okay. That'd be good."

We pass the wheat silos on the edge of town and Kat bends down to slide her bag out from under the seat in front. When her stop comes into view, Ronnie slows, then pulls off onto the gravel next to the little red car that's waiting there. Kat's house is only a ten-minute walk from here but her mum thinks kids should be met after school. She doesn't like the idea of Kat "running wild through the bush", which is pretty funny considering they barely live out of town.

Her mum winds the window down and waves. Kat grins as she hurries down the aisle. "See you, Fran-chess-ka!"

"See you." I wave back at her mum, trying not to

laugh. My name isn't Francesca. It's just Frankie. *Short for nothing but not good for nothing.* That's what Dad used to say. Yet no matter how many times I've told Kat's mum, she's never quite believed it. She says Francesca is a perfectly lovely name and it's a shame to shorten it and she's going to use it even if no one else does.

We swing back onto the highway and the radio crackles into static, the way it always does around here. Houses give way to farms and the smell of the ocean fades in the distance behind us. I settle back in my seat and rest my face against the window until — twenty-five minutes and three stops later — Ronnie drops Newt and me off at our corner.

We have to walk about a kilometre along the road and then through the bush up the steep dirt track we call a driveway. Newt reads the whole time, but I wait for him anyway. Because even though he's seven, which would normally be old enough to walk up a driveway by yourself, he's also absolutely and utterly Newtish. Which means he could easily get distracted and trip over a branch or a rabbit hole or possibly even his own feet.

When we finally get to the house, I take the key from the zip-up pocket in my bag. I slide it into the lock and jiggle it left, then right, then left with a twist.

"Bag!" I call as Newt slips past me. Then I sigh as he drops it on the floor and disappears down the hall.

A few seconds later I hear the door to his room close. He's working on some project in there, the same as always – not that I have any idea what it is. Mum and I have a deal with Newt that we don't go inside without what he calls "official advance notice". This is fine with us since his room's always crammed with weird stuff and you never know what you might step on or tip over or accidentally blow up.

I grab his bag and look through, checking for banana peels and apple cores and early signs of fungus. I check for notes and find yet another "absolutely final" reminder from Mrs Harris, the librarian, that *1001 Spectacular Science Facts for Junior Einsteins* is unacceptably overdue. I put that on the fridge at eye level where even Mum shouldn't be able to miss it.

Mum's a nurse at the hospital. She was taking time off when Newt was little, but after Dad died she had to go back to work. That was when Newt and I started going to Kat's. Back then, Mum used to come home so tired she'd fall asleep in her uniform.

She doesn't do that any more, but she still works hard. Even though she's meant to finish at four during the week she often ends up staying back, doing a bit extra. Which means I should probably think about dinner. We've had baked beans on toast twice already this week. Fish fingers and cheese once too.

If we were at Kat's, right now we'd be drinking milk and eating freshly baked biscuits. After that we'd watch *Gilligan's Island* and *Get Smart* on their colour TV and no one would have to get up and bang it because the picture kept turning into snow.

But if we were there, I wouldn't be able to make Newt's birthday cake. And that means he'd probably have to settle for a Swiss roll from the supermarket again. Mum always has grand plans to make him something special then at the last minute she runs out of time.

That's why this year I said to leave it to me.

It's not like I can make anything fancy but I know how to make cupcakes. And I know Newt.

Right now I'm glad that I planned this, because it's the perfect distraction, something to keep me from thinking about 1980 and high school, about Skylab and Dad.

Only what's that thing people say — that if you try not to think about a polar bear, the only thing you end up thinking about is a polar bear?

Don't not think about it, Frankie. Just make the cakes.

I get the flour and the sugar from the cupboard, the milk and butter from the fridge. I sift and crack and pour. I start.

Three

"Blow out the candles!"

On Saturday night we have Newt's birthday party. Only it isn't really his birthday and it isn't really a party. It isn't his birthday because that's on Tuesday but Mum's late so much on weekdays it's easier to have it now. And it isn't a party because Newt doesn't like crowds. So instead of a bunch of kids playing "pass the parcel", it's the three of us doing what we always do – cake, then presents, then leave Newt alone to assemble his presents, or take them apart, or maybe both, one after the other.

"Go on," Mum urges but Newt's too busy staring at his cakes.

"This is so cool!" he says. "I mean ... Mars would probably be more melted. And technically Saturn is made entirely of gas, but otherwise ..."

It was a simple idea. I made ten cupcakes in different sizes and icing colours. I wrapped black paper around Mum's big cutting board, drew some curving lines on it with Hobbytex paints and arranged the cakes in order. I cut out aluminium foil stars and scattered them everywhere, then put one candle on every cake except for the sun, because it makes plenty of light all by itself.

I didn't have to look anything up – not the order of the planets or which ones were bigger or even what colour they should be. Even though I haven't thought about space in ages, when I stared down at the cutting board, the whole solar system was there in my head, like a diagram in a book. Or like I was looking through the telescope on a cloudless night.

Clear skies, dark nights.

That's what Dad always hoped for. And I did too, when I waited for him at the top of the driveway, watching for flashes of our old purple Datsun turning homewards off the highway.

Those nights, everything would be right there in front of us. We'd put an eye to the telescope and the Milky Way would be a shining carpet, the ridges and bumps of the moon's surface so close I'd catch myself reaching out as if I could touch them.

My stomach twists with remembering. Then twists harder as I try to stop it. It's Newt's birthday. It's time for candles and cake and presents. *Don't think about a polar bear.*

I turn towards him, summoning a smile. "I'll blow them out myself if I have to!"

It takes him three puffs but he eventually covers all the planets. Of course, he refuses to make a wish, same as always, because he's a *scientist* and why would anyone believe in that kind of thing?

Mum pinches his cheek. "I can't believe you're turning eight. When did you get so big, anyway?"

"Actually," Newt says, "I'm quite small for my age. The average height for—"

Mum laughs. "You know what I mean."

We each eat one of the planets and then it's time for presents.

As Newt unwraps Mum's, I hold my breath.

Somehow she always seems to get things that aren't quite Newtish – the sort of beginner things you buy for someone who doesn't know anything about science. Last year she got a plastic microscope that broke the first time he tried to adjust the focus; the time before it was a book called *The Young Scientist's Guide to Absolutely Everything Worth Knowing*, which inexplicably failed to include a single word about quantum physics.

I'm not a hundred per cent sure this is why Newt put together his Big Birthday List but it seems likely. The list, which he's stuck to the side of the fridge, contains exactly forty-seven items. I don't know what Mum's bought but I'm sure of one thing: it won't be anything from the top ten.

Number one on Newt's list is a genuine dinosaur bone, preferably from a Tyrannosaurus rex, and number ten is a TRS-80 home computer. Some of the things in-between haven't even been invented yet.

"Number twenty-eight!" He starts grinning before the wrapping paper's even half off.

Mum sighs and I realise she's been holding her breath too.

Luckily, she doesn't see Newt's face change a few seconds later. It's the smallest flash of disappointment before he wipes it off and looks up at Mum.

"It's perfect!"

It isn't. What Mum's bought is a crystal radio, and what Newt wanted was a crystal radio *kit*, so he could build one himself.

"This is really great. Thanks." He folds the paper up neatly and studies the box, turning it over and over as if he needs to read every bit of it immediately.

I wait a few minutes, then reach under the table. "My turn!"

It's a present in four parts, each with its own package.

Since I only get fifty cents pocket money a week, there's no way I can get anything from Newt's list. Usually, I get him some comic books but this year I realised something.

That the best present for Newt isn't a thing – it's a project.

When he opens the first package he frowns. "Coathangers? Um ... thanks."

When he opens the second his frown gets deeper. "Aluminium foil? Okay."

He's trying so hard to act grateful I struggle to keep a straight face.

Then he opens the third one and his mouth opens in a little *O*.

This one has the instructions I wrote out with help from Mr Despotovski. He's a relief teacher who takes us sometimes when Mrs Easton's away. A couple of weeks ago, he told us you can make an antenna yourself with a few simple things. Straightaway I thought about our crackling TV and a few seconds later, I thought about Newt.

When Mr Despotovski saw how excited I was, he spent his whole lunchtime helping me do the instructions so they're just right – enough detail that Newt can do it himself, but not so much that it's too easy.

"Thanks, Frankie."

"You've missed one." I point at the wrapping paper he's moved aside. The last thin package has got caught up with the rubbish.

When he opens it his face brightens. "A notebook!"

Mum leans forwards. "What a clever idea."

Newt's always scribbling stuff everywhere – ideas he's had, interesting things he's seen, anything he might ever want to possibly remember. He writes them on scraps of paper and the backs of envelopes and in his school exercise books when he's meant to be doing spelling or maths or anything else at all. But when he gets serious, when he decides to really focus on something, it's different.

That's when he starts one of his notebooks. He writes a project name on the front and fills the inside with facts and figures and questions about that one thing only. Usually, he uses one of the old notebooks Mum has lying around. They're flimsy and cheap and they fall apart really quickly. But this is a special one I bought at the newsagent. It was seventy cents but it was worth it. It's got a sturdy cardboard cover and spiral binding.

On the front, I've written: **"INVESTIGATIONS INTO THE VIABILITY OF RUDIMENTARY ANTENNA CONSTRUCTION"**.

Mr Despotovski helped me with that bit too.

Kat said she wasn't sure "rudimentary" was a word, but when I checked the dictionary it was right there: *involving or limited to basic principles.*

Newt's got that look in his eyes. He grabs one of the coathangers and jumps up. "I'm going to start this now!"

Mum glances out the window. "It looks clear tonight.

Hey, why don't we watch *Disneyland*? It'll be like old times."

"That's on Sunday," I say.

And I'm too old for it, I don't say. *Plus Newt's more of a* Doctor Who *kid anyway.*

Not to mention that the old times you're thinking of were when he was too little to remember.

"Oh. Well, tomorrow then. I could do a roast as well … how about that?"

"Sure," I say. "That'd be great."

I know it won't happen. Mum's been promising us a roast for ages and she's always too late or too busy or too tired. It doesn't matter, though. Newt and I are fine. I can do four different things on toast and spaghetti bolognaise as well. Sometimes I even put the spaghetti bolognaise on the toast; it's my very own gourmet creation. I can also fry chops and sausages and pretty soon I'm going to teach myself to make apricot chicken using a packet of French onion soup like they do in *The Women's Weekly*. We don't need roasts, even if I do sometimes miss those crunchy potatoes Mum used to make.

"Hey!" Newt's twisted some wire around the coathanger and is holding it up, angling it this way and that. He hovers near the TV, trying to get a good look at the screen. "I think it's better already."

The news is on. The announcer, who Kat calls "Orange-Tie Man" because no matter what pattern they have, his ties are always the same colour, has his serious face on.

"At this stage," he says, "Skylab is anticipated to enter the Earth's atmosphere sometime between 15th June and 2nd July."

On the screen behind him is a picture of what looks like a huge metal windmill floating through space. I wonder if Kat's watching this. I wonder if it looks different in colour.

But most of all, I wonder if Mum's heart is pounding the way mine is, whether she's remembering that night in the Shack – the blanket and the photo, the sky full of stars.

Whether she's remembering Dad.

I sneak a glance at her but her face looks normal. Normal for her "News Face" anyway, the one she always makes right before she tells us to *turn it off, for goodness sake*! because all they ever talk about is doom and gloom and calamities on the other side of the world that have nothing to do with us.

"What is that thing?" As Newt leans forwards, the picture breaks up. Orange-Tie Man, who's actually Grey-Tie Man on our black-and-white set, dissolves into static.

At least the sound's okay. We're all quiet as we listen, as Orange-Tie Man tells us Skylab weighs approximately seventy-seven tonnes and is about the size of a small house. He says NASA doesn't know where the "wayward space giant" is going to come down but that the chances of anyone being hit are remote.

"Remote! Is that supposed to be reassuring?" Mum glances at Newt, as if she's suddenly remembered he's just a little kid. "There's nothing for us to worry about, of course."

Newt isn't worried. He's staring at the static-filled screen, his eyes shining.

"Space giant!" he breathes. "This is the best birthday present ever."

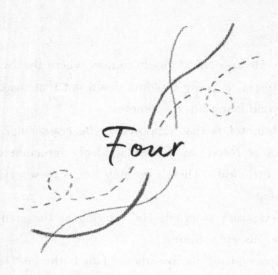

Four

The thing is, Skylab actually *was* Newt's birthday present, in a way.

Dad was so excited when he found out the date it was launching. "America's first space station!" he said. "Smack bang on his birthday!"

Right away, he decided it was going to be their special thing together. He'd start a Skylab scrapbook and when Newt got older, they'd track it and study it and learn everything there was to know about it.

"Isn't that a great idea?" he said, and I nodded, even though the idea of Dad and Newt doing special space things together made me feel a bit funny. My birthday was in February and nothing had launched then. But maybe there'd be something next year and even if there wasn't, Dad said not to worry.

"We'll still do our special things, short-for-nothing. And you can help with Skylab too, if you want."

I never did decide if I wanted to help. Newt was only two. He'd be doing little-kid stuff with Dad, not official real future astronomer things like me. I was going to think about it later. There was plenty of time.

"Space giant!" Mum's voice cuts across my thoughts. "Good grief, what next?" She goes over to the TV and presses the button. Orange-Tie Man snaps into focus for a second, as if he's teasing us, then dwindles to a fine point and disappears.

"Hey," Newt protests. "I was watching that!"

Mum stands in front of the screen, her arms folded. "We don't need all that doom and gloom tonight. It's meant to be a celebration! How about we check out the radio instead?"

Newt gets up and follows her back to the table. They sit opposite me and flick through the instruction booklet. Mum points things out and Newt pretends it's interesting and I stare past their heads at the spot where Orange-Tie Man was. Mum's words echo in my mind:

Doom and gloom. Nothing for us to worry about.

Hearing about Skylab — even seeing it — didn't mean anything to her. It's like she has no memory of that night at all.

Maybe it's better that way. *Easier.*

That's what she'd say, I reckon. It's what she said a few years ago when she took our family photos off the mantelpiece and tucked them away inside an album. *It'll be easier for all of us, love.* It wasn't like they were gone, she said. They just weren't right in front of us the whole time. We could get the album out whenever we wanted and look at them together.

I can't remember the last time we did that.

I get up and go over to the mantelpiece. There are other knick-knacks here now – vases and bits of pottery and craft projects from school that have taken up the space as if nothing else was ever there.

I look away, down towards the potbelly stove. Apart from the hot water bottles we take to bed at night, this old wood-fired stove is what keeps us warm over winter. There's a box next to it where we store kindling and newspapers. Mum doesn't buy the papers – because of the doom and gloom and all that – but she usually brings a pile home from work when they're too old for the waiting room. And seeing them now makes me think ... maybe we've got that article Jeremy was talking about.

I reach into the box and flick through. The headlines are yelling about the usual stuff – about *Arms Race Peril* and *Crisis Talks at the Kremlin!* Sometimes they mix things up a bit with *US Bases Shock!* or *Fuel Shortage Looms!*

Doom and gloom and calamities that have nothing to do with us. I suppose Mum's right about most of that stuff. None of it really touches us down here on the south coast of nowhere. What people mostly talk about is whether there's been enough rain, or too much, or the right amount of rain but at the wrong time, or ...

Wait. A word jumps out at me – a headline, if you can call it that. I stop flicking and peer closer.

Re-entry for Skylab.

It's hardly even an article. It's just a few short paragraphs, each little more than a line. And instead of being up front with *Crisis Talks!* and *Arms Race!*, it's a few pages further back.

It's basically what Orange-Tie Man said, about how NASA has no idea about anything but there's no reason to worry. Which is pretty pointless, if you ask me. If that's the best you can say, why say anything at all?

I suppose they'll know more later. The last line says *NASA will be constantly updating predictions on when Skylab will tumble out of orbit.*

Something about the word "tumble" makes me smile. It makes Skylab sound like it's a cartoon character, a cheerful space thing that's dropping by for a visit. For a second I picture it with chubby cheeks and a cheesy grin.

And isn't "re-entry" kind of strange too? It makes things sound all neat and tidy, like Skylab's going to knock and ask for permission. *Excuse me, but I seem to be falling and I was wondering ... would you mind terribly much if I landed in your general vicinity?*

I suppose it's because they don't want people to be afraid. The papers are always like that. They can make things sound however they want.

I remember when Dad was in the paper, when they said *Local Man Missing* and it sounded like he could have been anyone. When they said *Radio contact lost* and it sounded like all you needed to do was adjust an antenna and he'd be back again, right as rain.

Later, they said *Search abandoned. Hope lost.*

And even the full stops were loud then, like someone was slamming a door in my face, over and over.

In spite of myself, I turn towards the window. If you know where to look, you can still make out the Shack all the way up on the hill. Trees have grown around it, their scraggly branches hiding the front door, the "Welcome to the Universe!" sign Dad and I painted. It's faded and peeling, fallen sideways off its hook above the rusty padlock.

No one goes up there now. There's no point. With the telescope gone it isn't a Space Shack any more. It's just a broken-down shed with a hole in the roof.

"Frankie!"

Mum's voice makes me jump.

"I don't think we need a fire yet, love. Maybe you could come and help with the dishes."

"Okay." My voice feels unsteady, like I've been caught doing something I shouldn't.

I'm about to close the paper and drop it back into the box when something makes me stop. I slip the double page out and fold it – over and over until it's small enough to hide in the palm of my hand. Small enough to slip into the pocket of my jeans.

I don't know why I do it. I just do.

It's silly, I tell myself as I take a tea towel from Mum. I'll put it back later. It'll be cold enough for a fire after school soon and I'll need it then – to crumple up and stuff inside a tent of kindling, to set a flame to.

And that's what I'll do.

Definitely. Probably. Because Skylab falling has nothing to do with us.

Five

On Monday it's cold but sunny, the best kind of autumn day. At lunchtime Kat and I sit in our favourite spot on the bench outside the shelter shed.

"What's that brown stuff?" Kat points at my sandwich.

She's got a ham and salad roll. Her mum bakes the rolls at home, shaping the dough so there's a fancy little twist on top. I've got a cheese and Vegemite sandwich I slapped together about ten seconds before Newt and I made a dash for the bus.

And, apparently, some brown stuff.

I peer at it. "Maybe peanut butter?"

That's what I made for Newt; I must have forgotten to clean the knife before I did mine.

"Yuck! Why would your mum mix peanut butter and Vegemite?"

I shrug. Kat doesn't know Mum's usually either still asleep or already gone when Newt and I get up. Her mum insists we go to their house during the holidays, but as far as they know, we're only alone for an hour or so on school days, and a few extra on the weekend, the way it was when we first started staying home. Kat has no idea I make most of our lunches. And some of our dinners.

"It's actually pretty good." I take a bite. "Might be the next big thing."

"Very funny." She tosses a piece of crust to a magpie that's been stalking us.

I press my back against the corrugated iron, soaking up the warmth, and look out across the playground. We're supposed to finish eating before we do anything else but there are kids all over the place throwing balls and spinning skipping-ropes and playing elastics. On the other side of the assembly dots, the boys have already staked out the bat tennis and King Ball courts. If we want to play, we'll have to elbow our way in later. We used to do that all the time but lately we've stopped bothering.

"Oh, look out. Here comes trouble."

At first I think Kat means the magpie, but when I look up, Newt's weaving his way towards us, right through the middle of an intense game of Poison Ball.

"Look, Frankie!" It takes me a while to work out what he's holding. It's the radio Mum gave him — part of it, at least. He's taken it to pieces, stripping the wire off the drum and unscrewing something from the back.

"That was a birthday present, Newt. Don't wreck it!"

"I'm not!" He looks indignant. "I'm *analysing* it. It's *science*." Something crosses his face. "Oh, do you think Mum will mind?"

I sigh. "Don't worry about it. I'm sure it's fine."

Newt brightens. "This might be good wire for the antenna too. I wonder if I can swap some."

He wanders off, stepping through a game of jacks and narrowly avoiding a low-flying skipping-rope.

Kat shakes her head as a netball whizzes past his ear. "Sometimes I wonder how he survives."

"Yeah." I lick the last of the actually-quite-disgusting peanut-butter-Vegemite combo from my fingers. "Tell me about it."

* * *

When we go back in after lunch, there's writing on the blackboard.

STORM BOY PROJECT, it says. And underneath that:

WHAT is the story about? (Plot)

WHO is the story about? (Character)

WHERE does the story take place? (Setting)

DESCRIBE your favourite part.

DESCRIBE your least favourite part.

WHY do you feel that way?

Mrs Easton taps each line with her pointer.

Jeremy groans. "But that book is so dumb. I still don't get why we couldn't do the other one."

A couple of kids glance at me, then look away. They get it, even if Jeremy doesn't.

Storm Boy is the book we just finished reading in class. It's about a boy whose best friend is a pelican called Mr Percival. It's really good and nowhere near as weird as it sounds. Or maybe it's both those things. I don't see why it can't be.

"You should also," Mrs Easton goes on, "include one other aspect of the book you think is particularly worth exploring. And I want you to really give that some thought." She looks slowly around the room, her gaze resting on each desk in turn. "Remember, you'll be in high school next year."

She turns back to the board and adds:

Other Relevant Aspect

She looks pointedly in Jeremy's direction then underlines "Relevant" again.

"I'm giving you plenty of time." She picks up a piece of chalk. "I want you to show me what you can do." She turns to the blackboard and writes in the top right-hand corner: *STORM BOY* PROJECTS DUE 11th JUNE.

"Wow." Kat counts on her fingers. "That's practically a whole month!"

"It's also possible," Mrs Easton goes on, "that some people did not give the book their full attention during class and may want to consider reading it again."

This time, she doesn't even have to look at Jeremy. "But it was so boring!" he protests. "The only good bit was when the pelican got shot."

"Yeah, that was unreal!" adds Dale. "My uncle shoots ducks. I go with him sometimes. That Storm Boy kid is a total wuss."

"Quiet!" Mrs Easton taps the board so hard little puffs of chalk dust fly into the air. "*Storm Boy* is a beautiful book. An Australian classic. It was time for a change, that's all."

She looks everywhere but in my direction and I look out the window – at the playground, the flagpole, at everything but the sky.

It wasn't time for a change. Nothing ever changes around here. Year Six has been doing *To the Wild Sky* for as long as anyone can remember and we'd be doing it this year too, if it wasn't for me. I knew that even before Mrs Easton took a copy out to start reading. Before her eyes widened and she looked quickly up at me.

I'd already seen the cover, with its picture of a small plane crashed into water, and I knew there was no way we'd be reading that book. There was no way Mrs Easton would ever mention it again.

No one ever wants to talk about Dad. If they accidentally do, they start waving their hands. "I'm so sorry," they say. "I just didn't think."

I thought that was a good thing. *Easier*. Like putting the photos away.

But you can't put Skylab away. It's coming whether we like it or not.

And Dad's back in my head too, no matter what Mrs Easton does.

It's funny when you think about it – that she replaced a book about a plane crash with a book about a bird.

It's because she didn't know. Because she doesn't know.

And all at once I'm glad about that. I think about the knick-knacks on the mantelpiece and Mum staring at Skylab as if she's never seen it before and all I can think is that I wish people would talk about Dad.

I wish it more than anything in the world.

Things That Fall
From the Sky

Birds.

From the heat, sometimes. Up north, it gets so hot, birds fall clean at your feet.

I found a dead bird once. It was lying in the middle of a track in the bush, like it was waiting for me.

Mum said a feral cat must have got it, but there was no mark.

It looked perfect, like it was only resting.

What if a bird dies from old age, the way people die in their sleep? And they'd never know when they hit the ground. One minute flying, the next minute gone.

That would be all right, I think. That would be okay.

Planes.

People don't talk about that much, though. They don't want to alarm you.

Instead they say, *Relax and enjoy the flight. Watch the clouds from your window. Read a book and have a cup of tea. In the absolutely improbable and unlikely event of anything at all please use the inflatable slide.*

I've never been in a plane but Kat has, when she went to visit her grandparents in Sydney. She said the Earth was a patchwork of colours and the ocean was a bowl full of sky.

I wonder if that's what Dad saw.

He wouldn't have been reading a book or having a cup of tea. He would have been looking out the window the whole time. He had been in a plane before but not like this. It would be so different to being in a big plane, he said. He could hardly wait. There would be almost nothing between him and the sky.

I wonder if he saw the bird.

That's what did it, they said.

In the unlikely event of a bird breaking your windscreen ...

In the unlikely event of an uncontrolled descent ...

In the unlikely event of you crashing into the wide ocean ...

It was a tiny plane. It was bad luck. It was wrong place, wrong time, a one-in-a-million thing no one could ever have predicted.

They fell from the sky like a stone.

One minute flying, the next minute gone.

Six

On Friday I bring my sleepover stuff to school.

Newt brings his antenna kit. The coathanger hooks stick out of his bag like a weird art project.

"I don't think Mrs Blair is going to let you muck around with their TV," I say.

"Actually, I think she will."

He's probably right. Kat's mum's always been good about Newt's funny little projects, even when he shrank Samboy chip packets in her oven and made baking soda volcanoes on her nice clean floor. Kat's father is less enthusiastic, but we don't see much of him because he works such long hours. As well as his normal job, he's also the mayor, so he has lots of meetings and stuff.

Which is handy, because it gives Kat's mum time to air out the oven and mop the floor again.

As Newt gets off the bus, his bag swings wildly and I grab it just in time to keep the coathangers from spiking him in the arm.

Last thing in the afternoon Mrs Easton scans the room with that look in her eye.

I hope it's not me. It could be me. After the salad bowl incident, she said she's not going to tell us the day before any more. Now, she expects us all to be ready, just in case.

If it's me, what will I say?

I could be *a nurse because there are so many people who need helping and because it's important to give back.*

That's what Mum says sometimes when she comes home late and tired. So many people helped her when she needed it and now Newt and I are old enough to look after ourselves, she can help people right back.

I can't be a nurse. If I get up there and start talking about that, who knows what will come out of my mouth?

Next to me, Kat's sitting up straight and still. She's not looking at Mrs Easton. She's being perfect and right and at the same time pretending she doesn't care so Mrs Easton will think she's the one doing the choosing.

Kat's busting to have her turn, because if there's one thing she knows, it's exactly what she's going to do in the future. She knows what subjects she needs to study and where she's going for uni and the best spot for her office. It's going to be near the river in Perth, with a view out the window and a playground kids can use while they're waiting.

"Katrina?"

When Kat talks, she's clear and confident. She doesn't hesitate or stumble once. She makes everything sound so simple, so easy and perfect, that I almost want to be a paediatrician with an office by the river too.

Because the future depends on children, she says, *and because it's important to contribute to society.*

Mrs Easton beams. "Well, that was excellent. In fact, a perfect note to end the week on."

When Kat sits down, she's practically glowing.

"That was great!" I whisper. I'm happy for her. Of course I am.

But the truth is I feel something else too.

Jealous? Sad? It's neither of those things exactly, yet at the same time it's both, kind of mixed up together. Because I was so sure like that once. And not just me, but Dad too. He said I'd have to work hard if I wanted to be an official real astronomer but I could definitely do it.

"You have a good brain, Frankie-short-for-nothing," he said. "A good brain and a curious mind. And that's the best possible place to start."

That's why I was so excited when he told me about the astronomy convention. "All the way over in South Australia," he said, "and we're going!"

Only when he said "we", he didn't mean me. He meant him and his friend, in his friend's tiny plane, which only had enough room for the two of them and no extra space for a very small girl, not even if she begged and said she didn't mind sitting on Dad's lap and would be fine without a seatbelt.

It wasn't for kids, Dad said. It wouldn't be any fun for a small Frankie, not even one with a good brain and a curious mind. But when he got home, he'd tell me all about it.

And so he went, in that tiny plane, across the desert – and the ocean – and I stayed. And then he stayed gone.

For the longest time after that, just looking at the stars made me feel sick. Like the Earth and sky were swirling around me and I was the only thing standing still.

That's why I can't be an astronomer any more. Because I can't spend the rest of my life thinking about them. I just can't.

✦ ✴ ✦

Kat's still glowing when we get to her house. We sit at the table and her mum serves us tall glasses of milk and chocolate chip biscuits, warm from the oven. Newt wolfs

49

down three biscuits as if he hasn't eaten in days and then asks if he can borrow some wire. "Not plastic. Needs to be metal." He flips through his antenna notebook. "Copper, if you have it."

Kat's mum hurries out to the shed like she's been set an important challenge. As the door bangs behind her, Kat sighs and reaches for another biscuit. "I wish those talks were being marked."

I nod. "I reckon you'd definitely have got it."

Kat's on a mission this year. Because everyone in the school knows Mrs Easton doesn't give A-pluses, not ever. "A is the highest mark," she says, "and that's that."

But if anyone's going to make Mrs Easton break her rule, it's Kat. She always has amazing ideas for projects and she knows exactly what teachers like. Even in kindy, she used to print her name carefully on all her work and keep her pencils sharpened.

She drains her glass and wipes away her milk moustache. "So, do you want to work on yours?"

I hesitate. I don't really feel like thinking about it now, with jealous and sad all tangled up inside me. "I should be all right. I'll probably be a nurse or something."

"Oh, lovely!" Kat's mum comes in with a coil of wire. "Like your mother. Such important work, nursing."

Kat rolls her eyes and I smile back at her. "Seriously, don't worry. I'll work something out. Maybe we could ..."

Watch TV, I was going to say but Kat's already out of her chair.

"Oh, good," she says. "Because ... wait a sec." She goes down to her room and comes back with an armful of books. She spills the pile onto the table and retrieves a roll of pale blue cardboard from under her arm. Whenever we have a special project she gets one of these so she can do it like a poster.

"I really wanted to get started on that *Storm Boy* thing," she says. "I've got heaps of ideas."

I pick up a book. They're from the public library in town. This one's about seabirds. There are others about South Australia and fishing and coastal wetlands.

"You can borrow them if you want. Hey, I got you some cardboard too. Hang on."

She's back a minute later with another sheet of card. "I hope you don't mind white. I wasn't sure what colour you'd want."

"White's great, thanks. A blank canvas."

"Exactly!" She grins and starts leafing through one of the books.

While she takes notes, I go to my bag and get my copy of *Storm Boy*. When I flip to my bookmarked page and sit reading, Kat gives me a funny look.

"How come you're doing that? Wait ... don't tell me you didn't give it your *full attention during class*?"

She does the last bit in a Mrs Easton voice. It's scarily accurate.

I laugh. "I thought I'd have another look through it, so ..."

So I can read it properly, so the good bits aren't wrecked by Jeremy calling out things like, "Err, spew!" and "I wuv you, Mr Percival!".

"So I can think about that 'relevant aspect' thing," I finish.

"Oh, okay. I've already chosen mine. I'm going to do the life cycle of the pelican. I've got heaps of good information. No one else is going to have these books, either. You can borrow them if you want."

"Thanks."

Kat takes notes and I read. After a while Newt puts the TV on so he can test his antenna design. I don't know if this is what Mr Despotovski meant by "rudimentary" – from here, it just looks like a twisted bunch of wire. Then again, Newt could probably explain the angle of every twist if I asked.

I'm not going to ask.

We watch *I Dream of Jeannie* and then *Gilligan's Island*. Bits of them, at least, depending on what Newt's doing at the time.

When *Get Smart* starts, I look up at the clock on the wall. Mum should be here by now. Every time I hear a car I think it's going to turn and pull in but it's always someone going past.

At twenty past five the phone rings. It's out in the hall so I can't hear what's being said but after she hangs up, Kat's mum sticks her head in. "Slight change of plans. Your mother's going to meet us at the drive-in."

Kat frowns. "How come?"

"Something came up at the hospital. She needs to stay a bit longer." She nods at me reassuringly. "Such important work. I'm glad we can help."

Kat rolls her eyes again, but I don't feel like smiling this time.

Seven

After dinner we head straight to the drive-in so we can get a good spot. This is very important. You don't want to be so close you have to crane your neck all the time but you don't want to be right up the back either.

There's half an hour before the movie starts, so Kat and I go and hang out at the playground near the kiosk. Newt doesn't want to come — firstly because he doesn't like playgrounds and secondly because he's busy reading a week's worth of newspapers.

He spotted today's paper on the bench as we were leaving Kat's. It was the big photo of Skylab that caught his eye, the headline that read *Only Twenty Minutes to Duck*. When Kat's mum said he could bring it, he asked if they had any others and she grabbed them for him. Hopefully they'll keep him busy until Mum comes, save him trying to connect his coathangers to the speaker or something.

There's no one else at the playground so Kat and I go down the slide a few times and then sit on the swings. We glide lazily back and forth, trailing our feet through the sand. After a while she stands up on the seat and looks back towards the front gate.

"I wonder what time your mum will get here."

"Shouldn't be long," I say. Cars are coming in steadily now and the place is starting to fill up. It must be nearly 6.30.

Some little kids drift over and I can tell they want the swings. We jump off and steady the seats for them, then head to the kiosk.

"Reckon it's too cold for a choc-top?" I ask.

"Never."

"Medium popcorn and a choc-top, then." I hand over my one-dollar note, crumpling Queen Elizabeth between my fingers. I suppose it's a big deal, getting your picture on all the money, but it doesn't seem that great to me, having people buy stuff with your face.

I take my change and am shovelling coins into my pocket when it occurs to me. "Maybe I should get something for Newt."

Kat frowns. "He's not staying for the movie. For all we know he's already gone." She passes a two-dollar note across, asking for Fantales and a choc-top.

There are mixed lollies on the counter, already made up into bags. Ten cents and twenty cents. I've got enough.

"Come on." Kat takes her stuff and turns, already heading off. I hesitate, then follow. Newt's fussy about lollies anyway – when we go to the milk bar, he never buys the pre-made bags. He takes ages choosing and then goes back and forth endlessly, saying, *One of those and two of those and one of those, no, wait, maybe two* – until Mr Rayner's smile starts looking like it's been painted on.

As we approach the car, Kat slows. "I guess he's still here then."

The light's on inside and Newt's in the back seat with Kat's mum. She's knitting and he's flicking through the papers. There are some on the seat on either side of him – the papers on one side still sitting on the front page, the others folded open to pages on the inside.

"There's so much Skylab stuff!" he says when he sees me looking. "Hey, did you know that it was launched on my birthday?"

I turn my attention to a drip that's making its way down the side of my ice cream.

He picks up a sheet of paper from his pile. "It says the 14th of May but that was in America, which means the next day here, because of the time difference and everything. So it would actually have been the 15th for us."

I know all this, because Dad explained it. *Officially*, he said, it wasn't the same date. But *technically*, it was the same day. Which made it better. Which made it almost like a secret.

A secret it's taken Newt no time at all to work out. "Pretty cool, huh?"

"If you say so." I slide into the front passenger seat and nod back at the papers. "You can't just take those, you know."

The click clack of knitting needles stops. Kat's mother waves a hand. "Oh, that's fine. I said he can have them. They'll only be lining our bin otherwise."

Newt raises his eyebrows at me and I turn back to the front. Kat's in the driver's seat, working steadily on her choc-top. We won't start the Fantales or the popcorn until the movie has started. This is a rule that must never be broken.

It won't be long now. The spots around us are all taken and most people have settled in. The family next to us has reversed their station wagon in and put the tailgate down. The kids are lying in the back with pillows and blankets. It looks fun, sort of like camping, and for a second, I wish that was us. But then the big screen flickers to life and even though it's only the ads at first, I lean back and breathe out. It's almost my favourite part — this feeling you get when something's starting, when it's about to pick you up and carry you for a while and there's nothing you need to think about or worry about or ...

"LOOK OUT!"

There's a loud bang on the roof. I jump, bashing my knee on the glove box. Ice cream smears down my front and popcorn spills everywhere.

"What on Earth ...?" Kat's mother clutches at her chest.

Faces appear in the window. It's Jeremy and Dale, grinning.

"BOOM!" Jeremy says. "Skylab's coming!"

"Get lost!" Kat yells, but they're already backing up.

As they run off, laughing, I wipe ice cream off my shirt and try to salvage the popcorn.

"Unbelievable," Kat mutters.

"At least it was only the ads." As I speak, the screen goes blank. A few seconds later, dramatic music crackles through the speaker and the movie starts.

"The boys probably missed the first bit," Kat whispers.

"Serves them right."

Kat's mum turns around and glances towards the entry. "Gosh, your mother really is late, isn't she? It's lucky this happened tonight, when you're with me. Imagine if you two had been home by yourselves all this time."

I glance at Newt, but his attention is fixed on the screen.

"Yeah," I say. "Lucky."

We watch in silence for a bit, chasing drips on our choc-tops, dipping in and out of the popcorn.

On the screen a fireball rockets through the atmosphere and baby Superman crash-lands on Earth. He climbs out of the crater and holds out his arms.

"I wonder if that's what Skylab will look like," Kat says through a mouthful of popcorn.

"You mean with a baby climbing out of it?"

"I mean like a fiery rocket thing." She frowns. "But actually ... what *will* happen to the people in it? I mean, it's a space station, right?"

"It's not that kind of space station." Newt's face appears in the space between our seats. "That's only on TV – people in silver jumpsuits and space shuttles and stuff. No one lives up there. It was launched by a rocket and they control it by computer."

"Oh, okay. That's good."

"Astronauts have been there, though. I read something a minute ago ..." There's a rustle of paper as he reaches behind him. "Here it is. It says three crews have visited Skylab on Apollo spacecraft, spending a total of–"

"Not now, Newt," I whisper. "We're trying to watch."

"One hundred and seventy-one days on board," he finishes, without missing a beat. "They came back to Earth by splashdown, but not like Superman. Did you know–"

"Okay, Newt." I say. "We get it."

"Skylab's much bigger than Superman's spaceship too. Only he isn't Superman when he's in his spaceship because he hasn't started being a hero yet. He's Kal-El when he comes to Earth. That's his Krypton name. Did you know that, Frankie?"

Beside me, Kat stiffens and takes a deep breath.

"Just be quiet and watch." I lean in front of him so he has to sit back in order to see. He stops talking and I hear Kat exhale slowly.

About half an hour later, we're deep in the movie – seats back, stretched out. A noise has woken Clark Kent up in the middle of the night. He goes to the barn, where the remains of his spaceship are kept, and there's a strange light inside. It's a glowing green stick and he reaches down and down for it as the music swells and then ...

BANG!

There's another thump on the roof of the car. A blinding light shines in the window.

Kat moves fast. She jerks the door open and scrambles out, yelling. "I said GET LOST! GO AWAY!" Then her voice lowers. "Oh! Sorry, I thought–"

"QUIET!" someone calls from behind us. "We're trying to watch the movie."

"Yeah," someone else adds. "And sit down while you're at it!"

There's muttering from all sides, people flashing lights towards us.

"Sorry! I tripped!" It's a familiar voice now, a shape ducking down into the window. "So sorry," Mum says. "I didn't mean to startle you." She beckons to Newt. "You ready, love?"

By the time he gathers his stuff and gets out, then comes back twice because he forgot the newspapers and one of the coathangers fell out of his bag, we've missed a whole chunk of the movie and neither of us is sure exactly what's going on.

Kat sighs heavily as Newt disappears between the rows of cars for the third – and hopefully final – time.

"Sorry," I whisper. I know it's not my fault but it feels like it is.

Eight

The next day it's Mum who says sorry. She says it over and over.

She says it to Kat's mum when she and Newt come to pick me up.

"Oh, no problem at all!" Kat's mum waves her hands as if she's shooing away a fly. "I'm glad I could help."

She says it to me in the car on the way home.

When I don't reply, she says it again, then adds, "You know what it's like, love. There's always something that needs doing."

She wants me to tell her not to worry, that it's fine. And then she'll ruffle my hair and say how mature I am, that she doesn't know what she'd do without me.

Only I don't feel like hearing that stuff right now, so I turn my face to the window and sort of shrug instead.

After a while Mum stops apologising and keeps her eyes fixed on the road, and it's such a relief I almost feel guilty.

"Hey," Newt says as we head onto the highway. "Did you know that Skylab is the heaviest man-made object ever to orbit our planet?"

I glance into the back seat. He's brought the pile of papers with him from last night. I turn back, press my face against the window again. Not that there's anything much to see. *Tree*, I think. *Tree, tree, small bush, slightly larger bush, tree.*

"That satellite thing again?" Mum says.

"It's a space station," Newt says. "Only not like in the movies. Did you know that it was launched on my birthday?"

"Was it?" Mum smiles absently in the rear-view mirror.

"Technically but not officially." Newt rustles papers as if he's on urgent business. "Because of the international dateline and all that. Actually ..."

There's more, but I don't hear it because suddenly there's a break in *tree, tree, small bush, tree* — a sign flashing past, a turn-off coming up. It's the road that leads to the cemetery and there's nothing special about that. We pass it all the time, let it blur past without a second thought because why would you think twice about a road you're not taking?

Only it feels different now because all at once it hits me ... that it's today. May 19. The day Dad was on his way home in that tiny, unlucky plane.

Stop thinking, I tell myself. *Tree, tree, bush.*

It's not like the date means anything, anyway, because no one knows exactly when Dad died. Because even though they found the pilot, still strapped into his seat like he was fine and just having a little rest before he started the engine and took off again, they never found Dad.

Slightly larger tree, slightly smaller bush.

The second sign. The actual turn-off.

It flashes past. We flash past.

Mum doesn't even turn her head.

* * *

Later, Newt's in his room and Mum's gone to work and I'm sitting at the table. I've got out my pencil case and an exercise book and I should definitely be working on my Fantastic Futures talk and if I'm not doing that I should probably be starting on my *Storm Boy* project. And if I'm not doing either of those things I should be thinking about dinner because the last thing Mum said as she rushed out the door was that she'd meant to take a casserole out of the freezer but *sorry, love, is there any way you could do beans or spaghetti or maybe even that apricot chicken you've been talking about I think there's some chicken in the fridge but maybe give it a quick sniff test okay love you bye.*

Three choices. All I have to do is pick one.

Instead, I'm thinking about *tree, bush, road sign, turn-off.*

I'm trying not to think about a polar bear.

It's not that I want to go to the cemetery. We used to, but it was kind of a relief when we stopped. Everything about it had felt wrong somehow.

Maybe it was because we knew Dad wasn't really there. Because all we had was a silver plaque set in marble on the grass and nothing about it even felt like him.

Charles Avery

November 12, 1942 – May 19, 1973

For one thing, his name. No one ever called him Charles. He was always Charlie, if he wasn't Dad.

And for another, the date. Like someone just picked one and said, "That'll do."

Whoever did that, it wasn't us. It wasn't me.

"What are you looking at?"

Newt's in the doorway, a tangle of wire and coathangers in his hands.

I'm staring out the window, I realise, towards the top of the hill. But it's *tree, bush, tree* up there too. There's nothing to see.

I flick my gaze back to the table, to the books. "Nothing. Just thinking."

He goes over to the TV. "I have to test some things."

"Okay."

He fiddles with the knobs and the wire, stopping every now and then to write in his notebook. And I watch, pretending I'm not. I wish I could focus like Newt. Once he decides to do something, it's that one thing and nothing else. It's like he spins a little world and disappears inside it.

I push my chair back. I'll sort dinner out. That's what I'll do. Then I'll come back and make a start on *Storm Boy*. Or Fantastic Futures. One of them, for sure.

Except Newt's left the door to the hall open and as I walk past, the bookshelf catches my eye. The album, with the photos, with Dad.

The next thing I know, I'm sliding it out. There's a sucking noise as the plastic cover sticks to the books around it, but then it slips free. I sink to the carpet, cross-legged, my back against the wall between the bookshelf and the phone table. The album's on my lap. I watch my hands turn the pages.

Baby photos and little-kid photos and photos of the first house we lived in, a place I don't even remember. Then ... *oh*.

The mantelpiece photos, the ones Mum took down.

There he is, right there. There we are, all of us.

And I get it, I do. I understand why Mum put the photos away. Because looking at them makes you sad. It makes you think, *He was here and now he's gone.*

But the thing is, it makes you happy too.

It makes you think, *He was here.*

There's a sheet of plastic covering them, holding them down. I work my fingernail under the corner, peel it back. Am I just trying to see more clearly ... or maybe to touch them?

I trace my fingers over the photos, pick one up and hold it to the light. Another. Then ... this one, where Dad's roaring with laughter because he almost fell over trying to make it back before the timer went off and Newt's wriggling out of Mum's arms and she's lunging forwards, trying to grab him and I'm–

"Frankie!"

My hand freezes. Something crashes in the lounge room. The sound of something falling. Many somethings.

"Frankie! I need–"

I'm on my feet, shoving the album back onto the shelf.

I'm spinning on my heel, running into the lounge room.

"Oh, Newt."

He's okay. I mean, the cabinet near the window has half-fallen on him, but he seems to be holding it for now. He's at full stretch, his arms pushing back against it, his skinny legs braced.

Braced and trembling, actually.

He turns his head slightly. "Help?"

The photo's still in my hand. I slip it into my pocket and hurry over, taking the weight of the cabinet.

We push it back against the wall, bend down to pick things up off the floor. Books. An old clock. A vase. A complicated tangle of wire and coathangers.

I pick up the wire and look him in the eye. "What happened?"

He shrugs. "The antenna needs to be higher. I thought—"

"You were *climbing* it?"

"I didn't know it was going to fall over." He looks thoughtfully at the cabinet. "Maybe if I—"

"No," I say firmly. "No furniture climbing. Ever. Got it?"

He looks around the room. I can practically hear his brain searching for some technical loophole.

Finally, he nods. "No furniture. Got it."

I hold his gaze as I hand him the antenna. "Write it in your notebook. Don't forget."

Things That Fall
From the Sky

Newt, once.

It was the middle of the night, pitch dark. He was halfway up a tree, trying to climb higher. I was standing at the bottom, trying to make him come down.

It was no one's fault.

It wasn't Mum's fault. She was exhausted from work and slept with earplugs so nothing but her alarm could wake her.

It wasn't Newt's fault. He was only four and there was no way he could understand.

It wasn't Kat's mum's fault. She was trying to be kind when she told Newt Dad was watching over him from above, that when he looked up at night, Dad would be the brightest star, shining down on him.

She couldn't have known Newt would take it literally. That he'd start climbing hills and ladders and rooftops in the middle of the night, trying to get as close as he could to the sky.

If it was anyone's fault, it was mine. I had hidden the ladder but I couldn't hide the trees. Maybe I should have told Mum. I always meant to. I'd lead Newt back to the house, tuck him in and plan to tell her tomorrow.

But when morning came, I never did. Mum always seemed like she had enough to worry about already, with working all the time and those envelopes that kept arriving with red writing saying "Overdue" and "Final reminder".

So I didn't say anything — not to Mum and not to Newt. I didn't tell him Dad wasn't really a star. I didn't want to be the one to take that away from him. Instead, I started sleeping with my door open, listening for his footsteps in the hall.

That night, I didn't hear him until he was on the verandah. By then, it was too late to stop him climbing. All I could do was try to talk him back down.

When he fell, I caught him. Or at least, I broke his fall. He had the wind knocked out of him — and so did I — but he didn't break anything. He was okay. We both were. And so we could go back to bed, wake up in the morning, and pretend it was all a dream.

Nine

On Sunday two things happen.

Two and a half things, really.

The half is that when I get up, there's a note from Mum. It's on the bench in the kitchen, right where I always stand staring into the cupboards wondering what I should make for dinner.

"HOME BY 4.30!" it says. "DO NOT COOK!"

The next thing is that she actually does it. At 4.27 she comes through the door with a paper shopping bag in her arms and a big grin on her face.

"We're having steak and chips!" she says. "And apple crumble!"

Apple crumble! My mouth waters at the thought. The buttery, brown-sugary, coconutty thought.

Only ... the supermarket's closed on Sundays. The

bag Mum's holding is from the milk bar, but you can't get steak there, or potatoes, or apples. When she unpacks it onto the bench the only things inside are a small tub of vanilla ice cream and a bottle of lemonade.

Not that I'm complaining, but ...

Mum sees my confusion and laughs. She goes to the fridge and reaches into the very back, pulling out a plate with a thick piece of meat on it.

"Took it out of the freezer this morning," she says. Then she reaches up to the top cupboard, the one I can't open without standing on a chair, and gets down two bulging brown bags.

Granny Smiths and potatoes.

"Got them yesterday," she says. "See how organised I am?" She puts the bags on the bench, then opens a drawer and scrabbles around inside. "Still managed to forget the ice cream, though. Lucky the milk bar's open till five, hey?"

I nod, watching tiny bubbles fizz up through the lemonade.

"Now where's that peeler? I'd better get started on the spuds."

"Oh, here." It's in the dish drainer, where I left it last night, after the chicken failed the sniff test and I made sausages and vegies – peas and carrots and nothing else because we didn't have any potatoes.

But that was last night. Tonight, everything is different.

I grab the peeler and reach for the bag of potatoes. Mum waves me away. "Nope. My turn tonight." She takes the peeler from me, giving my hand a gentle squeeze. "I know how much you do around here, love. Don't think I don't see it. And I really am sorry about Friday."

That definitely counts as one whole thing.

＊

While she cooks, I sit and read *Storm Boy*. After a while Newt comes out with his coathangers and starts tinkering with the TV. He turns it on and off, switching between the two channels, taking a step back occasionally to frown and scratch his head.

At one point when I look up, the picture is worse than I've ever seen it. "Don't worry," Newt says. "It's science. Knowing what doesn't work helps you figure out what does."

I go back to reading. There's only a few pages left and I know what's coming. Part of me doesn't want to read it, but a bigger part of me knows it's really why I love the book.

"Can you hold this for me?" Newt calls. "It's hard doing everything at once."

I shake my head, keeping my eyes on the page. In the kitchen, hot oil sizzles as Mum drops fat wedges

73

of potato into the wire basket. She's about to start on the apples when she clicks her fingers. "Hang on – it's Sunday! That means *Disneyland*, right?"

I nod.

"Perfect!" She looks over at Newt. "It'd be good to have the picture looking a bit less ... *rudimentary* by then if you can manage it."

Newt shoots me a meaningful look. I sigh and close the book. For the next half an hour I'm his personal antenna-holding slave, bending the coathangers – and myself – all over the place like a game of Twister while he frowns and takes notes.

By the time dinner's ready, the picture's almost as good as it was before he started.

That's when the second thing happens.

Even though it's time for *Disneyland*, there's no sign of Tinkerbell. Instead, when we bring our plates into the lounge room, there are three men in suits sitting at a desk. They have papers and pointers and very serious faces. There's a TV screen behind them that says "SPECIAL REPORT" and a kind of easel between them with a photo of Skylab.

As we watch, one of the men unclips the photo and sets it on the desk. In its place on the easel is a large map of the world with a series of lines curving across it. The man closest to it taps the map with his pointer and starts talking about orbit paths.

"Did you know," Newt says, "that Skylab orbits the Earth 15.4 times per day?"

Mum frowns. "I thought *Disneyland* was—"

"Shhh!" Newt scoots closer until he's almost directly in front of the screen.

"At this stage it is expected to arrive sometime between 20th June and 4th July."

Mum frowns. "That's not what they said last time."

"That's because this is an update," Newt whispers.

Expected, I think. *Arrive*. Those words are for buses and trains, maybe babies. They're for things that have some sort of schedule, a timetable. Things that are cheerfully tumbling like cartoon characters, instead of plummeting towards us out of control.

Plummeting and plunging and crashing and …

Pointer-Man makes a spiralling motion, drawing Skylab down through the atmosphere, down through the sky towards the vast blue of ocean.

All at once it's a plane in my mind's eye. Dad and Skylab. Skylab and Dad. The whole tangled mess of it and I don't know how Mum can sit here and not see it.

I wish I could do that. I wish I could.

"It is estimated that the rogue satellite will strike the Earth in a path 160 kilometres wide and 6400 kilometres long."

Mum frowns. "How much is that in miles?"

"1.609 kilometres per mile," Newt mutters, his gaze fixed on the screen.

I wish I could sit here and focus on numbers and distances and grumble about why we had to change to the metric system anyway, like Mum's doing now, like she always does when someone says *kilometres* or *centimetres* when we have perfectly good miles and inches.

"I just don't see why they have to—"

"Shh!" Newt puts a finger to his lips and points at the screen.

"While most of Skylab will burn up on re-entry," says Other Pointer-Man, "it is likely several huge chunks will fall to Earth. Most will weigh less than four kilograms but several will be more than a tonne."

"A tonne!" Mum raises her eyebrows. "Good grief!"

"At this stage, NASA's Skylab Project Director says they are unable to offer advice as to what people should do when Skylab's re-entry is imminent."

"Right," Mum says. "Well, that's helpful of him."

"Don't worry," Newt says. "The odds of it hitting a populated area are very low. The Earth is over seventy per cent water, you know. Statistically speaking—"

Mum clicks her tongue. "Statistically speaking it's 6.37 and that means *Disneyland* should already have started."

"That's not statistics," Newt says. "That's time."

Luckily, before he has a chance to tell us all about the atomic clock and Greenwich Mean Time and who knows what else he's busy looking up in the filing cabinet inside his head, the serious-faced men sign off. Tinkerbell appears, scattering her fairy dust around the magical kingdom and Mum settles back against the couch. She looks from me to Newt and back again with a sigh.

"You kids," she says. "I'm just so lucky."

She leans over and ruffles my hair like she used to when I was little, and I let her, even though she's got greasy chip-fingers and is making tangles I'll have to tease out later with a comb.

"Next time I'll do a roast." She draws me in close, gives my shoulder a squeeze. "Still, this is pretty good, isn't it?"

And even though tonight's movie is *The Shaggy D.A.*, which I saw at the drive-in with Kat last year and was already too old for then, and even though there's a 77-tonne space giant getting ready to fall out of the sky who-knows-where-who-knows-when and who knows what you should do if it's anywhere in your general vicinity, I nod and snuggle deep into the cushions.

Because it is pretty good. It actually is.

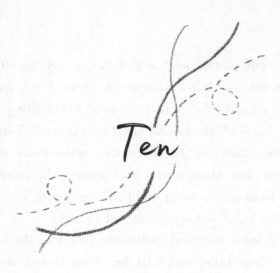

Ten

The next day Skylab is everywhere.

By which I mean that it's still up in space, quietly orbiting.

But it's also on the bus and in the playground and even in the toilets.

It turns out lots of people were on their couches at 6.37 wondering where Tinkerbell was, because at school, everyone's talking about Skylab.

They're saying *6400 kilometres!* and *How much is that in miles?* and *Huge chunks!* and *What does "imminent" mean?*

Some kids are looking nervously at the sky, like something could come plummeting down at any second.

Other kids are acting like it's no big deal, saying *NASA assures us there's no cause for alarm.* Saying *the odds of being hit are less than being struck by lightning.* Only when someone asks them what NASA stands for, or what the actual odds of being struck by lightning are, they have no idea.

Jeremy spends the morning banging his desk lid at random moments, trying to make us jump. "BOOM! SKYLAB!" he whisper-shouts, sniggering.

At recess the boys tell everyone about what happened at the drive-in.

"You should have seen them," Dale says. "They nearly hit the roof."

Jeremy laughs so hard chunks of chewed-up apple come flying out of his mouth.

For the rest of the week every time he sees us, he leaps into a Superman pose. "Look, up in the sky! It's a bird ... it's a plane ... no, it's SKYLAB!"

It is one hundred per cent hilarious. And one thousand per cent annoying.

Not just because it's stupid, and because getting chunks of someone else's chewed-up apple on your face is completely disgusting, but because it reminds me about the drive-in. It reminds Kat about the drive-in and I don't want her to think about that. About Mum and Newt and how wrong everything went. Kat said it was fine, but I could tell she was annoyed. When it's your best friend, you notice things without even meaning to.

We're okay, though. Kat and I don't ever really

fight. On Friday she brings in a couple of library books. There's one on wetlands and one about meteorology. "I've finished with these," she says. "You can have them."

"Thanks." I raise my eyebrows. "Um ... meteorology?"

She shrugs. "I thought there might be something about storms."

"But *Storm Boy* isn't really—"

"There's a storm in the book." She slides them across the desk. "You never know what's going to be useful."

I'm pretty sure these aren't going to be useful, but I take them anyway.

"I'll bring the rest next week," she says. "I should be finished on the weekend. I've got it all planned – look." She opens her desk lid and pulls out a sheet of paper. She's done a draft, a double-sided page with different sections and headings. "I'm going to do bubble writing for the main heading," she says, "with actual bubbles coming off it – because of the Coorong, you know? And then for this one I'm going to do the letters so they look like feathers." She grins. "I'm going to *make* Mrs Easton give me an A+. She'll be powerless."

"It looks great," I say.

"How's yours going? Have you worked out your relevant aspect yet?"

"Not quite. I'm still thinking about it."

It's sort of true, if you count thinking about thinking

about it and planning to do it very soon without delay and definitely without going back and reading my favourite parts of the book over and over again.

She frowns. "You'd better get moving. Remember, *you'll be in high school next year*! You have to *show her what you can do*." She does her Mrs Easton voice again, grinning. It's the same as before but for some reason this time it sounds annoying.

Also, I think, *we're supposed to really give it some thought.* That's what I'm doing, isn't it?

"I know," I say. "I will. Thanks for the books." And then I put them inside my desk where I will absolutely not forget to get them later.

*   *   *

Last thing in the afternoon Mrs Easton starts looking around, and I sit perfectly still.

I try not to blink. Then I wonder whether it's weird not to blink, whether that'll actually attract her attention, so I blink over and over really fast to make up for it.

I could be a journalist, I think. *I could be Lois Lane at the* Daily Planet.

Because I like writing stories. Because I like playing with words.

Only then I'd have to twist them, wouldn't I? I'd have to bend them into strange and unnatural shapes.

Expected. Arrive. Tumble.

I don't think I want to do that. I don't think I know how to.

Luckily, I don't have to. Because it's Sharon, today, and Dale.

Sharon is going to be a teacher, *because I want to be just like you, Mrs Easton, only even more than Jenny and also because ... I forgot.*

Dale borrows Jeremy's puffy jacket and Kat groans. "Not another astronaut!"

"Can't be," I say. "No salad bowl."

Turns out I'm right.

Dale isn't going to be an astronaut. He's going to work for the CIA.

"Only not really *for* them," he says. "More like a double agent."

Because someone has to get to the bottom of what the government's up to.

Because my uncle says the conspiracies go to the highest level.

Mrs Easton sighs. "And the jacket?"

"Because you have to meet your contacts in cold places. You always have to talk outside, away from bugs. Sometimes in Siberia."

"I see. And what exactly do you mean by conspiracies?"

"Like the so-called 'space race'." Dale makes air quotes with his fingers. "It isn't even real! My uncle said it's all a massive scam. Did you know they've never even been to the moon? They filmed the whole thing in a TV studio."

"Did they really?" Mrs Easton looks like she can't decide whether to laugh or cry. "Why would they do that?"

"To distract us!" Dale lowers his voice, as if he's worried the government might be listening, as if he suddenly wants to go outside, maybe even to Siberia. "From the real stuff, like the arms race and how we're all going to be fried and blown up and—"

"This uncle of yours," Mrs Easton cuts in, fixing Dale with a look. "He's a scientist, I suppose? An expert of some sort?"

Dale looks confused. "Nah, he's a farmer."

"Then I think we've heard quite enough."

"But—"

"No 'buts'." Mrs Easton does the air quotes now. "Come up with something else, please. I'll be calling on you again soon."

* * *

When we get home the house is cold. Cold enough for a fire, I think.

There's plenty of wood and heaps of paper in the potbelly box. Newt's been going through everything

83

looking for Skylab stuff but I made him return the bits he didn't want. Even if Mum doesn't bring any more home for a while, we'll have enough to keep us going.

I set up the kindling, then grab a sheet off the top. I scrunch it up and stuff it inside, then light a match.

The flame takes hold, curling the edges of the paper and then eating its way through the tightly spaced lines. *All that doom and gloom* flakes into ash before my eyes, along with the weather, the footy scores, an ad for *Superman* at the drive-in, and ...

I yank at the paper, pulling it back out. I let it fall to the floor, then stamp on it. A headline stares up at me, only slightly blackened.

Global Effort to Keep Skylab in Orbit.

It's weird that Newt missed this. At least that's what I think until I peer closer, and see why.

He wouldn't have bothered looking here, because this isn't the normal news section. This is what Dad used to call the weird and wonderful section.

It's where you find articles like *Confused Duck Thinks it's a Dog* and *Hapless Burglars Lock Themselves Inside Store.*

When I read this one, I laugh out loud.

On Wednesday next week, at precisely 1.05 pm, sixty-five radio stations all over the world are going to run a special "meditation broadcast" and they want as many people as possible to tune in. Even if you can't, you're encouraged to *focus your thoughts skywards* for seven and a half minutes on one thing only – lifting Skylab up.

This worldwide effort is being coordinated from America by the Brookline Institute for Psycho Energetics, which sounds like something made up for a TV show. Only they're real, and despite the fact they have exactly five members and their headquarters is probably in someone's lounge room, they're hoping to get over a million people. According to their calculations, if they get that many, they'll have a decent shot. I don't know what their calculations are based on, but they seem pretty confident. Their spokesman says this is a "bona fide science experiment" and if they can push Skylab 170 kilometres higher there will be no chance of it falling, ever.

The Skylab Project Director doesn't sound quite as confident. When asked for comment, he said simply, "Well, I hope they can help us out."

I glance down the hall, where Newt is shut away in his room. Would he want to read this? Especially since it's bona fide science and everything.

I can practically hear him now. *Actually, this is ridiculous! Did you know this is ridiculous?*

I fix up my kindling tent and shove the paper back inside.

If anyone does this, it'll be people on the other side

of the world; they'll be at work or school, or maybe on their lunch break or something. They won't be sound asleep like people here on the south coast of nowhere, Western Australia, where it'll be 1.05 am, twelve hours in the future.

Technically. Officially. Because of the international dateline and all that.

Except no one's really going to do it, are they?

Of course they're not.

I strike another match and this time I watch through the little window until the flame takes over, until the words crumble into ash.

Eleven

12.55.

The red dots on my bedside clock stare directly at me.

What am I doing?

It's Wednesday night. Thursday morning. Somewhere on the other side of the world a million people, or at least five, are getting ready to *focus their thoughts skywards*.

Right here, on this side of the world, I'm getting ready to join them. The thing is – once it was in my head I couldn't get it out, no matter how much I polar-beared. Because what if they get a million people but they need a million and one? What if my brain is the one that makes all the difference?

So before I went to bed, I set my alarm. Ridiculous. But still.

I look out the window. It's an ink-dark sky, alive

with stars. I throw a jacket on over my pyjamas, slide my feet into slippers. A few minutes later I'm outside in the night, sitting on the flat rock on top of the hill. It's wet with dew but my jacket is long enough to sit on.

Unless I climb a tree, this is the highest point for miles. I know it doesn't make sense but none of this does, and it feels like something – to be as close as possible, to be out here under the stars.

I flash the torch on and check my watch. 1.02. As the second hand speeds around the dial, my heart starts to race. Should I start at 1.05 to the second? Isn't every clock different anyway? Without the broadcast, how will I know when to start and stop?

1.03.

I'll start when I start. Even if it isn't exactly the same as everyone else, it'll be close.

1.04.

Wait. Would it be better to close my eyes or look up at the stars? Maybe I should be sitting in some kind of meditation pose. Maybe ...

The second hand ticks over and I start.

I put a picture of Skylab in my mind and stare hard at it. I close my eyes so I can't see anything else, and then slowly, slowly, I imagine pushing it upwards. I watch it move in my mind's eye and it almost feels exciting, like I'm really doing something, and I wonder if everyone else — all one million and one or possibly just six of us — is feeling this too.

I sit and imagine and watch and feel and after a while I start to wonder how long has passed and whether I should open my eyes and check the clock. And then I wonder who decided on seven and a half minutes anyway because it feels like an oddly specific length of time and maybe the sort of thing you'd come up with if you wanted something to sound more sciencey than it actually is.

When I open my eyes, it's 1.14. I've done two extra minutes and I don't know if that's good, bad, or nothing at all. Whatever it is, it's over.

And now that it is, I feel silly. I should go back to bed. It's cold out here and in spite of my jacket the damp is seeping through my pyjamas.

As I head for the path, something strikes me. This is the first time I've walked it alone at night. Before, there was always Dad, holding my hand. I remember our matching yellow gumboots and the way I used to watch our feet — one big pair, one small — picking their way down the rough trail.

I turn and look along the ridge. The Shack squats at the end like an old man bent against the wind. And then I'm walking, watching my one pair of feet, and then I'm there, standing beside it.

The door is padlocked and the lock is rusted shut. But

none of that matters because I'm not going in. I'm just ... I don't know. I'm just here. Pressing a hand to the wood, peering through the narrow gaps between the boards.

It's much darker inside. There are no windows and the light from my torch is weak. But it doesn't matter because there's nothing to see from here anyway. The corner directly in front is where the telescope used to sit – the Celestron Orange Tube C8 that was Dad's pride and joy. The empty space looks all wrong, like a mouth with the front teeth knocked out.

"Frankie?"

I jump, feeling a sharp pain as my palm snags on the splintery wood. When I turn, Newt's coming towards me across the ridge. No coat, no slippers, shivering in his *Doctor Who* pyjamas.

"What are you doing?"

"Nothing." I step back and towards him, standing between him and the Shack. "I ... I couldn't sleep."

"So you came out in the freezing cold to sit on top of a hill?"

I open my mouth, then close it again.

He grins. "You were doing that psycho thing, weren't you?"

I feel my face flush and am glad of the dark. He did know about it, then. I suppose he left the article in the box because he didn't need that one, because it was ridiculous.

"Well, how come you're awake?" I retort. "Don't tell me *you* were doing that psycho thing?"

He gives a little snort. "I'm awake because I heard your alarm go off. Then I saw your torch up here, so ..."

"It was dumb," I say. "I was about to come back anyway."

"Didn't look like it." He steps neatly past me and peers in towards the Shack. He doesn't have a torch, though, and I swing mine away so he can't see inside.

"Come on." I grab his arm. "It's late."

Surprisingly, he doesn't argue. He lets me spin him around, then he walks ahead of me back along the ridge. We're about to start down the slope when he stops and looks up. It's a clear night and the sky is a carpet of stars.

Skylab's up there somewhere, invisibly orbiting.

"I wonder if you moved it," he says. "I wonder if you've saved us all."

"Very funny." I nod towards the house. "Back to bed."

He's turning when suddenly he points back at the Shack. "Hey! Did you see that?"

"What?"

"There was a shooting star. Right over the top there."

"No," I say. "I missed it. Let's go."

I shine the torch on the ground and watch our feet

pick their way down the path. One big pair, one small.

And when I'm sure he's not looking, I turn around – just for a second – in case there's any lingering glow of light.

Things That Fall
From the Sky

Shooting stars.

Technically, I suppose they're really falling from space. Is space the sky? I'm pretty sure it isn't. An astronomer would know that.

Maybe I knew that, once.

Stars die in a beautiful blaze, leaving a fiery trail behind them.

That's what people say. That's what I've seen on TV, but never in real life.

There's no trick to it, Dad always said. All you have to do is choose one patch of sky and keep watching.

You'll see one, short-for-nothing. Trust me on this.

I never have, though.

When I was little, I used to stare until my eyes watered, then blink at the exact wrong moment, just as everyone else said, *Oh!*

I've seen flashes in the corner of my eye that made me turn my head, made me wonder.

But I've never been sure.

It doesn't count unless you are. Unless you're so sure

about that blazing trail you want to jump up and yell, "Hey! Did you see that?"

That's when you know you've been lucky. That's when you get a wish.

Newt hates it when people talk about wishing on stars.

"Stars are already amazing," he says. "*Science* is amazing. Why do people have to try to make it all magical?"

I wonder if I'd make a wish. It feels like it would be a shame to miss that chance. But there's only one thing I'd want to wish for, and it would be the one thing I know could never come true.

So what would be the point?

Maybe it's better that I never see one, so I don't have to decide.

Twelve

Twelve million people.

That's how many they got.

Twelve million.

Plus me, maybe. I don't know how they counted. How could they possibly include people who got up at the last minute and sat on a hill on the other side of the world?

But anyway, they got a lot. And it didn't make any difference at all. Skylab didn't move one single centimetre. Why would it? The news is laughing about it. People who did it are laughing about it. They never really believed it would work. Of course they didn't!

Maybe I'd be laughing too if I wasn't so tired. I don't know how many hours of sleep I got but it wasn't enough. In class, I'm trying to focus my bleary eyes on the board when Rachel puts her hand up.

"Mrs Easton," she says, "shouldn't we be doing duck and cover or something?"

Mrs Easton frowns. "I beg your pardon?"

"Duck and cover. It's when you hide under your desk and kind of curl up. Mum told me about it. It's for nuclear bombs but it might work for Skylab too."

"I'm not sure ducking is what's needed," Mrs Easton says. "In any case—"

"It was in the newspaper!" Rachel protests. "They said we'd have twenty minutes' warning. To *duck*. That's what it said and Mum reckons you're meant to practise at school, so—"

"BOOM!" Jeremy bangs the lid of his desk. "SKYLAB!"

Rachel jumps and Dale laughs. "Forget about ducking! My uncle knows where there's an underground bunker, out near the desert. It's from the war or something. There's enough room for ten people." He stands and starts pointing around the room. "Eeny, meeny, miney, mo ..."

"In England, people are going to hide in smugglers' caves," Jeremy adds. "Have we got any of those around here?"

"We have caves," Dale says. "Maybe not the smuggling kind, though. Is that important?"

Mrs Easton raps her ruler on the blackboard. "That's

enough, thank you. There will be no need for anyone to hide anywhere. The news likes to make things sound dramatic, that's all. My husband says there is no danger to us whatsoever."

"Good old Merv." Dale sniggers.

Mrs Easton shoots him a warning glance.

Merv is her husband's name. Dale knows this because his dad volunteers for the State Emergency Service, which is where Merv works. I know this because once when a tree branch came down on our carport, they came out and pulled it off with a truck and a chain, yelling, "Heave ho, Merv!" and "Go easy, Brian!" while Mum watched nervously.

"Hmmm." Jeremy strokes his chin. "This Merv of yours ... he's a scientist, I suppose? An expert of some sort?"

Mrs Easton gives him the blackest look you've ever seen and hands out a maths worksheet.

* * *

That night I dream about ducks who live in an underground bunker. They're scared of smugglers or the sky or something else I can't quite put my finger on. They're trying to lie low until the danger passes, but the bunker is made out of desks, and someone keeps opening the lid.

Dale's face stares down at them. "Only room for

ten!" he chants in a singsong voice, as if they're all just playing. "Eeny, meeny, miney—"

An alarm blasts me awake. I fumble for the clock, jabbing at the button.

12.55. I groan. I can't believe I forgot to turn it off. I was tired all day from last night; now tomorrow — today, actually — is going to be worse.

I roll back towards the window, willing myself to sink back into sleep. And my eyes are closing when I see the light. A star, blurring in the corner of my vision?

Then I see it again — a flash of something up on the hill.

It's a swinging light, too low to be a star. Too steady to be anything other than what it is.

A torch. Up on the hill. Inside the Shack.

I don't stop to put on shoes. I don't grab a jacket or a torch. I just run.

One of the boards has been twisted off its nails and pushed aside. Newt's made a gap for himself, wide enough to squeeze through, to edge his way in.

Wide enough for me to peer quietly through, to see.

He's sitting at the table, surrounded by papers. He scans them in the torchlight, pausing every now and then to shake off dust or cobwebs. He's on the taller of the two stools but he looks so little, like a kid who's finally been allowed to sit at the grown-ups' table. His white hair is fuzzed up from sleep in what we used to call his "mad-professor" look.

I stand there for a long few seconds, then take a deep breath. "Hey, Newt."

If it was me, I'd jump in fright, but he doesn't move at all.

"What are you doing?" I whisper. "You can't be up here."

He leans across and reaches for another pile of papers.

The gap is narrow but I manage to scrape through. I won't look around, I tell myself. I won't even breathe in if I can help it – the old smells, the memories. I'll get Newt out and then snap the board back into place behind us.

But as soon as I'm inside, he swings the torch, illuminating one corner after another.

"Look at all this." He says it as if it's a discovery he's made. As if this place isn't as familiar as home to me.

It's thick with cobwebs and dust but the Shack is still the Shack. It's tiny yet it never felt cramped. It felt like the exact right size for the thing it was made for, which was sitting quietly and looking at the stars. There are shelves along one wall, the small table and stools pushed up against another. And there's more room than there used to be, now the telescope's gone. Only the retractable roof is still here, the pulley system with the crank handle. Dad could have automated it but he liked turning it himself, watching the roof open inch by inch.

I liked that too.

"I can't believe all this stuff's here." Newt waves a hand and in spite of myself, I look.

The photos and diagrams and star charts, the newsletters and flyers Dad used to have sent from all over the world. The pages of handwritten and typewritten notes he made — we made — about what we'd seen and what we were going to see and when we were going to see it.

Everything's laid out exactly as he left it. Why would he bother putting it away? He was going to be back before we knew it.

Newt looks up. "I thought this place was empty. I thought that guy took everything."

"What guy?"

"I don't know. A guy. He came with a ute and then Mum ran inside crying."

I swallow. Newt was four when Mum sold the telescope. I didn't think he'd remember any of that.

The guy who bought it was so excited, said his kids were mad about space and they were going to love it. Then he looked at me and Newt and asked Mum why she was selling it, and she put her hand over her mouth and ran into the house.

After a while the man turned to me and said, "Well, maybe I'll give you the money, then?" and I nodded. I can still feel him counting fifty-dollar notes into my hand, my fist curling tightly around them so they wouldn't blow away.

"I didn't know you remembered," I say. "You were so little. I thought ..."

"I remember things."

For a second there's something on his face I can't read.

"Newt," I say quietly. "Do you ever want to talk about Dad?"

He shakes his head. "It makes Mum sad."

"Yeah, but ... that's not what I asked."

He holds my gaze and doesn't reply.

"That guy only bought the telescope," I say finally. "Everything else was just ..."

"Just left here. Sitting here all this time." He fans out some pages, sending dust flying. "Sputnik, Apollo, the moon landing."

As he pulls the page clear, the edges flake away beneath his fingers like old paint, crumbling onto the table. Crumbling and ... crawling?

"Newt!" I lunge, sweeping the top few pages onto the floor, the spider along with them. It scuttles between papers as it lands and I stamp down hard with my foot, squishing its black body, its red stripe, beneath the faded type.

"Hey!" he protests.

"That was a redback!"

"Oh." He reaches for the papers, spider guts and all.

And something catches in my throat, because there on one of the pages is my name in wobbly little-kid letters.

SPESHAL SPACE REPORT BY FRANKIE JEAN AVERY APRIL 1972

It's only a quick flash in the torchlight, but it's enough. More than enough. I can almost see my five-year-old self sitting right here at the table.

I almost *am* my five-year-old self. The years drop away suddenly like they were nothing. Like if I turned around, Dad would be right there, his hand on the lever, getting ready to fill the sky with stars.

I press my thumb against my palm, feeling a bump where the sliver of wood broke off last night. "It isn't safe in here, Newt. There are spiders and splinters and rusty nails and ..."

Memories. Even though I don't say that, sometimes they feel like the most dangerous thing of all.

"There's even stuff about Skylab. There's a picture here from years ago." He holds up a page and squints at it. "I *think* this says '1973'. It's a bit hard to read now because of the spider goop." He frowns at me like I'm somehow to blame for saving his life. "I'll try to clean it later."

"What do you mean 'later'? I told you – you can't be up here."

"I'll take this stuff to my room then. I can look at it better there anyway."

There's no point saying no. If I don't let him take it, he'll come back, which would probably be worse.

Plus, it's my fault he's here in the first place. I'm the one who came up to do that psycho thing, who stood here peering inside, as if there was something worth seeing.

If it wasn't for me, Newt would be tucked up in bed fast asleep.

It's not like it matters anyway. It's just Newt being Newtish. There's a giant space thing falling from the sky and he's found a secret stash of papers. Of course he wants to read them. Of course he does.

It's got nothing to do with Dad. Newt doesn't know Skylab was meant to be their special thing. How could he? Memories are my problem, not his. And maybe in a strange sort of way, this is a good thing, a perfect thing.

Because Newt never got to have Skylab before and now he does, just a little.

Maybe the only things I need to protect him from are spiders and nails, a splinter or two.

I work my thumbnail along the ridge in my palm and the sliver slips free, as easy as anything. When I hold my hand to the light I can hardly even see where it broke the skin. It's the tiniest hole. It'll heal in no time.

Thirteen

"No," says Mrs Easton. "No, no, no." That's a lot of "no"s, but Dale deserves every single one.

It's Wednesday the following week. Our *Storm Boy* projects are due on Monday and Mrs Easton's given us some class time to work on them.

"To finish them off," is what she actually said, but I think Kat's the only one who's even close to doing that.

While we work, Mrs Easton's been coming around asking what we've chosen for our relevant aspect. I was racing to come up with an idea – something that would sound impressive, even just for now – when she got to Dale and stopped dead.

"Absolutely not," she says, folding her arms.

"Duck hunting is relevant!" Dale protests. "And I know heaps about it."

Mrs Easton turns and strides to the front of the room. "It seems that many of you are struggling with this project." She picks up the blackboard duster. "Based on what I've seen, it's clear some of you have a bit more thinking to do."

Her gaze sweeps the class, resting briefly on certain kids – Dale and Jeremy, Sharon, Marcus. Then she rubs out "11th JUNE" and writes "18th JUNE" in its place.

"I'm giving you an extra week," she says. "And that is absolutely final."

Next to me, Kat sighs. "She didn't even look at mine." She smooths a hand across her poster, which is spread out neatly on the desk in front of us. On the front, she's drawn a big picture of Mr Percival. All around him are neatly ruled sections with fancy headings. The bubbles she's drawn are kind of shiny and her feather writing somehow looks almost like actual feathers. I have to stop myself from reaching out and touching it.

She hasn't finished the back yet, but I know she's got it all planned out.

"Never mind," I say. "That'll make it a bigger surprise later."

She looks thoughtful, then nods slowly. "Maybe it'll give me an even better chance of getting an A+!"

"Yeah." I close my notebook and tuck it away inside my desk. "I reckon."

After school I really try. I force myself to sit at the table, looking through Kat's books and taking notes. I do it the next day too, and all weekend.

Well, not *all* weekend. Most. A lot. Not counting the times I get up to hang the washing or check on Newt or make lunch, and then dinner, now Mum's gone back to working late again. It was different for a few days, but then things went back to normal. I guess she only had a limited amount of sorry. I guess she ran out of *knowing how much you do around here, love, don't think I don't see it.*

She's busy. I know that. It's work. And the truth is, the washing and the cooking and the Newt-ing aren't the reason I can't seem to get started.

I don't know what the reason is. I only know I don't want to use any of these notes. I don't want to use any of these books. I keep going back to *Storm Boy*, staring at the cover, picking it up, reading my favourite bits over and over again.

The part where Mr Percival comes back.

The part where Storm Boy runs across the dunes, calling.

The part where they make the Lookout Mr Percival's place forever.

This book. Just this one. I can't help thinking that

everything that matters — everything that *should* matter — is right here.

On Sunday night I'm chewing my pen at the table while Mum cleans up in the kitchen. The TV's on but no one's watching it. Mum made Newt change the channel as soon as she got home — from the *doom and gloom* news to *Disneyland* — so he put the antenna down after a few minutes and disappeared into his room.

There was nothing about Skylab tonight, anyway. There hasn't been for a few days. I suppose they need to take a break from saying, *We have no idea what's going on but don't worry!*

Mum grabs a sponge and starts wiping the bench, sweeping crumbs from the baked beans on toast into her cupped hand. She glances at the abandoned TV and sighs. "Well, Newt's certainly keeping himself busy, isn't he?"

I nod.

"That antenna project was a great idea, love." She tips the crumbs into the bin and squeezes the sponge out over the sink. "He doesn't seem that taken with the radio. I thought it was what he wanted, but ..."

"It was," I say. "It is. You know Newt. He likes to focus on one thing at a time."

As I hear myself say this, I wonder if that's true right

now. He's working on the antenna but he's following Skylab as well. Maybe Skylab doesn't really count as a project, though. All he's doing is reading about it, and if he doesn't do that now, if he waits until he's finished his Rudimentary Antenna Design, it will have landed, or *arrived* or *re-entered* or whatever it is they're calling it.

"You're right." Mum smiles as she comes over to wipe the table. "He's just so ... Newty, isn't he?"

"Newty?"

"Isn't that what you always say?"

"Oh. You mean Newtish."

"That's it! I knew it was something like that."

I pick up *Storm Boy* so she can wipe underneath it.

"You've been reading that a lot lately," she says. "For school, is it?"

"Yeah."

"Any good?"

"Yeah."

"What's it about?" She gestures at the cover. "A pelican?"

I hesitate. People are always asking that about books: *What's it about?* It sounds like a simple question, but it isn't. You could take all day to answer it if you really wanted to. And if the person asking the question really wanted to hear it.

"Yeah," I say finally. "It's about a pelican."

A pelican, I think when Kat shows me her poster the next morning. She finished everything over the weekend. She seems to have made her bubble writing even bubblier, if that's possible, and she's completely filled the back of the poster. There's a big section on the life cycle of the pelican, with diagrams, and a smaller one called "Habits and Habitat".

"Alliteration," she whispers. "Teachers love it. You can use that if you want."

I stare down at her anatomically correct pelicans. They look like the kind of drawings you find in books. "Thanks."

A shape looms over us from behind. Jeremy. "Is that your thing?" he asks. "Can I see?"

Kat rolls her poster up quickly. "I'm handing it in." She glances at the door to the classroom. The bell should be going any second.

"I'm not going to copy you!" Jeremy says. "I've nearly finished too — see?"

The bell goes as he opens the lid of his desk and pulls out a tattered sheet of cardboard. It's a weird brown colour and for a second I wonder why he chose that instead of blue or green or plain white, but when he holds it up, I realise it's because he's used the back of a Weeties box. The brown makes it hard to read the orange and purple texta he's used and I don't think he did a draft first, because there are a bunch of cross-outs where he's changed his mind about things. And a bunch of other things that probably should be crossed out. Under "Setting", which he's spelled with only one "t", he's written:

Storm Boy lives on the beach and doesn't wear shoes. He is a real ratbag weirdo. If I saw him I would give him a Chinese burn or put him in a headlock. Probably both.

"Shouldn't that be under 'Character'?" Kat says. "What have you got for—"

She leans forwards but Jeremy pulls the cardboard away and climbs up onto his desk.

"Character," he says loudly. "By Jeremy Ricardo." Then he clears his throat, which is probably why he doesn't hear Mrs Easton come in behind him.

"Storm Boy loves a pelican," he reads. "This doesn't make any sense. Ferrets are much better. If it had to be a bird, I would choose an eagle. Also, what is Storm Boy's actual name? How come the pelicans have names and Storm Boy doesn't? Another thing that doesn't make sense. In conclusion, this book does not have good characters. In conclusion, I rest my case."

"Down," Mrs Easton says, in a low, dangerous-sounding voice. "Now."

While Jeremy scrambles, Kat walks quietly to the front and puts her poster on Mrs Easton's desk.

Mrs Easton somehow manages to smile at Kat and scowl at Jeremy at exactly the same time. She taps the blackboard. "Remember, this is absolutely finally due in one week. Some of you are going well and others ... have a bit of work to do."

Jeremy tosses the cardboard into his desk and drops the lid loudly. "I don't get the point of this anyway. Why can't we do useful stuff?"

"Yeah, like learning how to survive the nuclear winter," Dale says. "And dodging massive space giants that fall from the sky."

Jeremy nods. "Hey, has Merv organised any sirens? In Belgium, they're going to sound a thousand air-raid sirens to warn people. In Switzerland, they're going to ring all the church bells. Hey, I could ring the school bell if you want. It's a big responsibility but I'm up for it."

Mrs Easton sends Jeremy out to beat the dusters, even though Heather did it last thing Friday and no one's used the blackboard since then. Then she writes some long division sums up and tells us to work in pairs.

"I can't believe people are worried about this," Kat whispers while we add the six and carry the one. "Dad says someone called the council to ask about evacuation shelters."

"What did he say?"

She shrugs. "What do you think? That NASA has everything under control."

"But that's not really true, is it? I mean, if it was under control it wouldn't be falling in the first place."

"Dad said they can correct it if it looks like it's going to land somewhere populated." She clicks the tab on her pen to switch colours. "It's not like they're going to let anyone get hurt, Frankie."

"But what if ..."

I don't bother finishing my thought. Because as I look at Kat I realise something. That nothing bad has ever really happened to her. She doesn't know things can change at any moment, that the bottom can drop out of the world. And that's a good thing. Of course it is. I wish I didn't know that, either.

"What if what?"

I press down hard and the lead in my pencil snaps. In a flash, Kat passes me her sharpener, and I take it. "Nothing," I say. "You're probably right."

Fourteen

At home I jiggle the key and clean out Newt's bag.

I start the fire, then check the cupboards for baked beans.

We've got three tins, plus two of spaghetti. We're fine.

I unzip my bag and tip everything out. Kat gave me the rest of the library books today and as they spread across the table, her words are in my head.

It's not like they're going to let anyone get hurt, Frankie.

That's the thing. When nothing goes wrong, you think it never will. The future looks like a smooth road that will just unroll in front of you.

You think you can make plans – to be a paediatrician or a teacher or an astronomer.

You think all you have to do is decide where you want to go.

Dad had plans. He was going to be home in a few days, with space souvenirs and stories to tell.

I blink, something prickling at the corner of my eyes.

I was angry when he left. I didn't want him to go without me. So when he came into my room early in the morning to say goodbye, I pretended to be asleep. I didn't roll over and give him a hug. I didn't do anything.

I think he knew I was awake. He stroked my head, leaned down and whispered in my ear. *See you soon, short-for-nothing.*

Soon.

I blink again and the room swims around me.

When the phone rings, I'm glad. I know it'll be Mum saying she's going to be late again, but it's something to do and I run to grab it.

"Don't worry." I don't even bother with "Hello". "I'll do beans for dinner."

"Um, what?" It's Kat's voice on the other end. "Frankie?"

"Sorry." I think quickly. "I was talking to Newt."

"Oh, okay. So listen, I know you've been stuck on your *Storm Boy* thing, and I had some ideas that might—"

The door to Newt's room flies open with a bang. He charges down the hall, his eyes widening when he sees me on the floor. He leaps over me like I'm a hurdle and runs past into the lounge room. The front door slams and I hear his feet crunch on the gravel. I stretch the curly phone cord as far as I can around the corner but I can't see him.

"Frankie?"

"I'm here," I say. "I—"

"So I was thinking – if you go to that book on river systems, there's a bunch of stuff about ..." She pauses. "Can you hear me?"

"Hang on," I blurt. "I need to ... hang on."

I drop the receiver and run outside.

There's no sign of him. And then I look up at the hill, tracing the path along the ridge to the Shack.

"Newt!" I yell as I head up the slope. "Get out of there!"

But there's no answer and when I reach the Shack, I see why.

He's not there. I turn back towards the house. And I freeze.

There's a ladder leaning against the wall around the side, past the carport.

Newt's on the roof.

I don't yell.

I don't do anything that might startle him. I hurry to the edge of the house, to the bottom of the ladder.

I make sure it's steady and then I climb up.

Newt's wobbling across the roof with his arms outstretched. In one hand he's holding a piece of wire — coathangers twisted into different angles, shining from the aluminium foil wrapped around them. He's heading straight for the old antenna on the very top.

I hold my breath and bite my tongue. Dad let me up here with him once when he was painting the roof. He said it was safe as long as you stayed low and walked on the joins.

Newt is not staying low. He is not walking on the joins.

He makes it anyway. He sits down and I breathe a sigh of relief. Then he turns his head and sees me.

He grins and holds up his coathanger contraption.

"That was for inside!" I don't know why I'm whispering, but I am.

"We need one up here too. Just wait." After some fiddling, he reaches up and attaches the coathanger to the top of the roof. "Hey, can you go and turn the TV on? I'll move this and you yell out when the picture's clear."

"I'm not going anywhere until you get down." I stay on the ladder, my hands gripping the edge of the gutter.

Newt bends the coathangers. Every now and then he looks out towards the hill as if he's checking something, measuring.

Every time he moves, my breath catches. Will this be the moment he stumbles? Which way will he fall? What will I do?

I'm turning these thoughts over and over when I see a flash of purple out on the highway.

It's early for Mum, though. Maybe it's someone else.

But how many purple cars are there? How many that come this way, that turn slowly off the highway and down our road?

"Newt!" My heart thumps like a hammer in my chest.

"All right, I'm coming!"

"Hurry up!"

I shouldn't have said that. He was fine until I did, scooting along on his bottom, actually staying low. But now he looks up and sees my face. And follows my gaze.

"Is that ...?"

He loses his balance and suddenly he's tumbling, pitching towards me.

All I can do is hang on and brace myself.

When he hits me, the top of the ladder bounces. I fling myself against it, pushing it back against the gutter. It wobbles, slides sideways for an awful second, then stops. Steadies.

One of Newt's feet is in my face. The other one is hanging off the edge. "Phew!" he says, like he's had some kind of cartoon near-miss. "That was close."

By the time Mum pulls in, we're back inside, both breathing a bit hard, but not so she'll notice.

Newt's got the TV on and is studying the picture. A couple of times, I catch him looking thoughtfully at the ceiling. First chance I get, I'm going to hide that ladder. Maybe I'll chop it up for firewood just to be safe.

* * *

It's not until after dinner that I remember the phone.

I run to the hall and scoop up the receiver, pressing it stupidly to my ear as if Kat might still be there, talking about wetlands and meteorology.

Instead, it beeps at me, making that dead sound you get when the phone's been off the hook for too long. I press the button down, holding it for a few seconds so I'll get the dial tone back, so I can call Kat and explain.

That's what I'm about to do when I notice the photo album. It's squeezed in with the cookbooks, instead of on the next shelf up, where it belongs. I must have put it back in the wrong spot when I ran to help Newt that day. I pull it out from between *The Australian Women's Weekly Cookbook* and a spiral-bound menu planner, but then I wonder why I'm even bothering to move it when no one ever looks at it. When I'm not looking now, even though it's right here in my hand because Mum's home and what if she sees? Because it's *easier* this way but we'll definitely sit and do it one day, all together, don't worry.

Just not today.

I slide the album back between the cookbooks and take my finger off the button on the phone. The dial tone beeps and I stare at the receiver. I should call Kat back and explain, say sorry.

Only I can't, not now. I can't listen to her talk about bubble writing and alliteration and how I should decide what to do and then go ahead and do it.

Like nothing could ever go wrong. I wonder what it would be like to believe that.

I drop the receiver back onto the cradle. And then I go to my room and get out two things.

Firstly, the photo. The one I slipped into my pocket while I was getting the cabinet off Newt, and then tucked under my pillow telling myself I'd put it back later – definitely, probably.

Dad took much better photos that day, but he put this one up on the mantelpiece right next to them. He said life was full of mess and mistakes and there was no point trying to hide it.

I set the photo on my desk where I can see it and then I get out the second thing – my copy of *Storm Boy*.

I don't open another book or take any notes. I don't do any headings or sections.

I just start writing.

Storm Boy *is about death*, I write. *It's about life, too. And love.*

Once I get started, I can't stop. Thoughts tumble out of me, one after another, as if they've been waiting behind a wall.

Death is about both those things. It's about life and love. If there was no death those things wouldn't matter.

I don't know where it comes from but it feels strange and right at the same time, kind of like the book.

Storm Boy isn't about a pelican. It's about losing something important, something that feels like a part of your heart. It's about things falling from the sky while all you can do is watch. About not being able to save the thing you love no matter how fast you run, no matter how much you hope.

Things That Fall
From the Sky

Rescue.

I used to think that's how it would happen, for Dad.

He'd cling to driftwood or a life-preserver, then wash up on an island. He'd be tired and thirsty, but he'd be okay.

He'd spell out HELP in stones and wait. He'd start a fire and wave his shirt and a rescue plane would spot him.

Only they can't land there. Maybe it's too sandy or rocky. You need a runway for a plane, even a small one. You need a safe space for a helicopter, a landing spot.

Maybe they have to send a boat for him. Maybe he has to wait a little longer.

So what they do is fly low; they lean out the window and give him a big thumbs up saying, "It's okay, mate! We've got you. We'll be back!"

Before they leave, they drop stuff for him, things he can use while he's waiting – food and water, warm clothes, a tarp or a tent, all of it bundled up tight.

It falls from the sky and it saves him.

He's rescued then. He's safe and everything is going to be fine.

That's how I thought it would happen, for the longest time.

Fifteen

In the morning, I say sorry to Kat. I say sorry on the bus and during class and at play lunch.

"I waited for ages," she says. "You said to hang on."

"I know. It was because of Newt. I had to–"

"Isn't it always?"

At least that's what I think she says. It's pouring today and it feels like the whole school is crammed into the shelter shed. Rain drums on the corrugated iron roof and a hundred voices bounce back and forth off the walls.

I lean in towards her. "What?"

"Never mind." Kat presses her Vita-Weats together, pushing tiny worms of butter through the holes. "It's fine."

"No, what were you–?"

There's a loud thump nearby. The shelter shed walls rattle like something's slammed into them and the bench vibrates beneath us. Jeremy's jumped up onto it and is standing in the corner.

"Roll up, roll up!" he yells, like a circus ringmaster. "Get your very own Skylab Protective Helmet here!"

"Only six available," adds Dale. He passes something up to Jeremy, who puts it on his head. It's a kind of bowl-shaped hat with a pointy spike on top.

"Save your head!" Jeremy yells. "Save your*self*."

A bunch of kids gather around, jostling and craning for a look.

"This is a joke, right?" someone says.

"No joke!" Jeremy taps the helmet. "They're selling these in America. My uncle sent them over. Because he cares about my survival."

Dale nods. "Place a bid now if you want to live!"

"Don't rely on the SES," Jeremy adds. "Merv hasn't even organised any sirens."

Kat rolls her eyes and shuffles further down the bench.

"As if it's going to come anywhere near us!" someone scoffs.

"Actually, you never know. There's an orbit path right over Western Australia."

I know that voice. I peer into the crowd and see

Newt's fair head, there in the middle. Which is not at all Newtish. The only time he puts himself in a group is when he accidentally wanders through one on the way to somewhere else.

"But you can't protect yourself with a helmet," he goes on. "Even if only a tiny piece hits you, the velocity would—"

"Excuse me," Jeremy booms. "These have been specially designed for Maximum Skylab Protective Power!"

This time I'm the one who rolls my eyes. I'm turning away to follow Kat when Newt says something else.

"Huge fragments of the American space laboratory will crash to Earth at speeds of up to 270 miles per hour, approximating the force of a dying meteor."

It's not what he says, but the way he says it. As if he's reading from something.

I edge closer to the group.

"With Skylab having seventy-one different orbit paths," he goes on, "there is no way of being certain where debris will fall until the last couple of hours."

He *is* reading. From the newspaper, maybe? One of the articles he got from Kat's place. It's a bit weird for him to be carrying them around, though.

"NASA advises that the best place to shelter is in a car, a house, or an apartment."

Nervous laughter ripples around me. "What about

schools?" someone mutters. "Do they count?"

I press forwards. At first I can only see flashes between people's shoulders and elbows, then a gap opens and I realise Newt's holding a notebook.

A notebook? But this can't be a project. He already has one. And anyway, there's nothing to work out about Skylab. There's nothing anyone can do except wait.

"What if we're at school?" A thin, wobbly voice comes from my left. A little kid, I reckon. "What if we're outside doing sport and—"

"That's exactly where your helmet comes in!" Jeremy reaches up to pat the pointy bit. "This important feature is the 'Early Warning Spike'. If a chunk of Skylab hits it, you'll get .00193 nanoseconds of warning, giving you plenty of time to jump out of the way."

"A nanosecond?" someone scoffs. "How long *is* that?"

Newt sighs. "A billionth of a second."

"A billion seconds!" Jeremy yells. "That's heaps. How many minutes is that, Dale?"

"Heaps!"

Newt shakes his head. "That isn't what I—"

"Listen, mate." Jeremy stares down at him. "If you want to walk around bareheaded while an out-of-control space station crashes towards you, go for it." He turns back to the crowd. "Anyone who actually wants to buy a genuine not-at-all-available-in-Australia

Skylab Protective Helmet, come and talk to me."

"Some assembly required," Dale adds quickly.

Some assembly turns out to mean cutting and folding and sticky taping. The so-called helmets are made of cardboard. They come flat in a poster with dotted lines on it.

I doubt there'll be any takers but plenty of kids hang around for a look.

I don't. I've got no idea why Newt's started a Skylab notebook but it's not like it can hurt him. Unless you count paper cuts, which are pretty low on my list of Newtish things to worry about.

I grab my stuff from the bench and go down to join Kat. As I flop down beside her, I grin. "Did you hear that?"

"How could I? I'm all the way over here. And you're all the way over there, watching Newt. Again."

This time there's no mistaking what she says. It's not only that Jeremy's stopped yelling and the rain has eased a bit. It's that when she speaks, she leans close and looks me right in the eye.

"He's my brother," I say. "I have to—"

"He's *eight*. You don't have to look after him every second."

"I ... you know what he's like."

Of course she does. Her place was practically our

second home for years. If there's anyone outside our family who knows Newt, it's Kat and her mum.

She almost scoffs. "He's not a baby, Frankie."

"I know that. It's just ..." I take a deep breath. "I'm sorry about last night," I say again. "I'm really, really sorry. I mean it."

"I know. You said. But it's not only that. It's the drive-in, and the last time you couldn't come over. And the time before that and when you couldn't come camping with us at the last minute and I had to play card games in a tent with Mum and Dad for five days." She hesitates, like she's making up her mind about something. "And whenever you *can* do something, he has to come too."

My mouth feels dry. Has she been thinking this the whole time? Is this a fight? It feels like it is.

"It's not that I don't like him." She glances down at the corner, where Newt's trying to explain about something called terminal velocity. "I mean, how can you not like him? He's so ... Newtish. He shrunk a Samboy chip packet for me — chicken flavour and everything." She sighs. "I just wish it could be the two of us sometimes, you know? You and me."

"Yeah," I say. "Me too."

I don't know if that's the truth or not. It's not something I've ever thought about, not something I've ever been able to think about. Newt's just always there, on the edge of everything. He has to be.

"You should come over sometime," I say. "To my place."

"It's all right." Kat twists a piece of plastic wrap around her finger. "You don't have to—"

"You can sleep over too!" My heart's pounding. I don't know why I said that. Or maybe I do. Hopefully I can talk Mum into it.

"Okay." Kat nods slowly. "That'd be good."

"Newt won't get in our way, I promise. He'll hang out in his room."

When he's not on the roof. Or in the Shack. Or . . .

"It's all right," Kat says. "He doesn't have to do that. I didn't mean . . ."

She smiles and I feel myself breathe out. We're not fighting. It was like a storm that went through. Or a sun shower, one that's over almost by the time you've noticed it's raining.

"I really am sorry about yesterday."

She bumps her shoulder against mine. "Yeah, I got that. It's okay, really. It was just this idea I had about *Storm Boy*."

I bump her right back. "Oh, guess what? I did it last night."

"Which bit? Do you mean the setting, because that's what I—"

"The whole thing. I've finished."

"Finished? I thought you were stuck."

"I was. And then I wasn't. So I did it. Actually, what you said really helped me."

It's true, just probably not how she thinks. It's like all that thinking about what I didn't want to do eventually made me realise what I did.

"Wow. That's great. Did you bring it? I can have a look at lunchtime if you want."

Usually, I show things like this to Kat. Even when I think I've finished something, she sees stuff I've missed. She helps me fix the headings, adds a few quick texta strokes that make everything look somehow neater or fancier.

She likes doing it and I like having it done.

But something about this is different. This morning, when I thought about her seeing what I did last night, I felt strange. Nervous. That's why I waited until she went to the toilet, then grabbed it from my bag and handed it in.

"Oh," she says when I tell her now. "Well, I'm glad you got it done."

"Yeah. All I have to do now is Fantastic Futures."

Kat nods. "At least you know you're safe on Friday."

"Yeah." We're not doing it this week because Mrs Easton decided to give us more class time to finish off *Storm Boy*. And I've been lucky the last couple of weeks.

My blinking technique seems to be working so far. We've had farmers and teachers and a vet, *because I like animals and because last year my dog got bitten by a snake*, but Mrs Easton hasn't looked like choosing me once.

"So, when do you want me to come over?" Kat asks.

"Not sure. I'll have to check with Mum."

"Okay." She grins. "Can't wait."

"Me neither."

Sixteen

We have to, though.

Wait, I mean.

Because when I ask Mum if Kat can sleep over, Mum says, "Yes, what a great idea!" but then frowns. "I'm just not sure when."

It's because of work, of course. She wants to make sure she's here and not running late. And I want that too, so when she says weekends are too hard at the moment and it'll probably have to be a Thursday or maybe a Wednesday but she can't be sure until the new roster comes out, I say fine.

Luckily, Kat's fine with it too. When I explain, she shrugs. "No hurry. Mum said I can come any time. You know what she's like."

When I tell her it probably can't be a weekend, she

shrugs again. "Doesn't matter. We'll still have plenty of time."

It's true. Mum will let us stay up late and watch TV anyway. I'll make sure the picture's clear. I'll get all the coathangers out of my cupboard if I have to. Or we can play games. There's a shelf in the hall cupboard that's full of them. We've got Yahtzee and Uno and Twister.

No, not Twister. We won't play that because it needs three people. And we're going to be two. Newt can do his own thing, with his antenna and his Skylab notebook and whatever other things he's decided to work on even if there are three or four and it's completely unfocused in a not-at-all Newtish way because it's not like it matters, does it? For one night I'm not going to worry about him at all.

* * *

One day after school I decide to get the games out. It's ages since we've played them. I'd better read up on the rules, make sure we still have all the pieces.

I go down the hall and scrabble around in the cupboard. It's a bit of a mess, with big things piled on small things, threatening to topple at any moment. The games are on the top shelf, right at the very back. To reach the Yahtzee box, I have to balance on the bottom shelf and stretch one arm up and out as far as it will go.

Somehow I manage to do it without knocking anything else over. I half-turn and am stepping down onto the carpet, when something moves near my foot. I can't see it clearly at first but the way it's crawling makes me draw back. And then I realise what it is — a redback spider coming from the direction of Newt's room.

My feet are bare because I took my muddy shoes off at the door. I can't step on it but I don't want it to get away, to disappear somewhere into the cracks of the house. So I do the only thing I can — I swing my arm down and squish it with a corner of the box.

The word "Yahtzee" now has a disgusting smear across it and so does part of the carpet. I'll deal with that later. Now, I grab the bug spray and go to Newt's room. I knock then turn the knob without waiting for a reply.

"Hey!" As the door opens, he looks up from his desk. "You don't have official advance notice! You can't—"

"There are spiders in here." I step inside. "We have to ..."

Suddenly all I can do is stare. I'm a cartoon character, my jaw dropped wide open.

Newt's room is like a scene from one of those TV cop shows, where the maverick detective gets obsessed with a case and sticks things all over the walls, trying to piece together the mystery.

There are diagrams of Skylab and the solar system.

There are star charts and maps of the Earth's surface, with curved lines circling and crisscrossing each other. Some of it is stuff from the Shack and some of it is newer, things Newt's drawn himself. There are pages of facts and figures written out in his careful handwriting.

"Newt, what is all this? What are you doing?"

He stares at me like this is the dumbest question he's ever heard. "Skylab stuff."

"I can see that. I mean how come it's all up here like ...?"

"I'm working something out. I need to be able to see everything."

I turn around slowly. There's a lot of everything.

He's got articles from the newspaper, too. He's cut them out, put them up. One whole wall is almost completely covered in them.

Skylab Keeps Jittery World Guessing

New Window for Skylab Re-entry

The Skylab Odds

But these aren't from our papers. Some are from the last few days, ones Mum hasn't brought home yet.

I look Newt in the eye. "Where did you get these?"

"From the library at school." He looks almost smug. "Pretty good idea, hey?"

"Those are for everyone to use. You're not supposed to cut things out."

He shrugs. "If anyone wants them, I'll put them back."

"That's not the point." Still, I can't help wanting to look. I step closer to the wall.

There's stuff about the smugglers' caves and the air-raid sirens, about Switzerland and the church bells. Nothing about bunkers or duck and cover or Mrs Easton's husband Merv.

At least not so far.

In the corner near the cupboard there are some weird ones. The president of India says Skylab is a demon and only God can save us. A woman in California says she had a dream that a satellite would hit a city called Perth. Two of her previous dreams have come true.

"See," Newt says. "You're not the only one who believes in that psychic stuff."

"I don't ..." I begin, but then I stop. There's another article here, tucked almost out of sight, a headline so small it's barely a whisper.

The Mystery of the Missing Plane.

For a second, all the breath goes out of me. But this isn't about Dad.

It's about a man whose plane disappeared last year over Bass Strait. It says he radioed in to say something was hovering above him, "playing some sort of game". Then there was a strange noise and he vanished from the face of the Earth.

I don't read the rest. I don't know what this is doing here. It's got nothing to do with Skylab. Maybe Newt's next project is going to be UFOs or something.

I watch as he gets up and goes over to one of the maps on the wall. He peers at it, then glances down at something in his hand. A notebook. I sidle closer but he flips it shut. There's a single word on the cover, staring up at me in thick black letters.

He's underlined it three times, added a fat exclamation mark.

SKYLAB!

At once, I remember the other day in the shelter shed. Newt reading from a notebook, about an orbit path going right over us. A little kid with a wobbly voice worrying about where to shelter.

Newt is only eight. It's easy to forget that sometimes.

I turn towards him. "Newt, are you worried about Skylab?"

"Worried?" He looks puzzled. "Why would I be worried?"

"You know, about being hit or something."

He does a little snort-laugh. "No."

"Well, what are you working out then?"

"I don't know. I haven't worked it out yet." He lowers his voice, as if he's about to share a secret. "You know how I said my birthday is the same as Skylab's?"

"Yeah, you and a million other people."

"Actually," he says, "it's probably more than a million. Statistically speaking. There are approximately four billion people in the world and three hundred and sixty-five days in a year, so ..."

"Exactly. So ... no big deal."

He hesitates for a second. He looks like he's weighing something up, deciding. When he finally speaks, his voice is quieter still. "Only I bet no one else has something like this."

He reaches into the drawer of his desk and pulls out a sheet of paper. It isn't a newspaper article. It's not a diagram or a map. This looks like the front page of a school project – one someone started and never got around to finishing.

Something deep inside me twists.

I've never seen this before but I know exactly what it is.

I knew Dad was going to do it, that he planned to. I just didn't realise he'd started.

Up the top, it says *Skylab, launched 15/4/73* and down the bottom it says *Isaac "Newt" Avery, born 15/4/71*. In-between are two black rectangles drawn up like frames. Inside one is a picture of Skylab. And inside the other is a photo. The one Mum took that night.

Dad at the telescope, Newt in a blanket.

Dad never saw this, though. It wasn't developed until months after he left.

What he did was leave a blank space, for later.

It's Newt who's filled it. Newt who went to the bookshelf and got the photo, then put the album back in the wrong spot.

He's watching me, waiting.

"Dad was going to make a scrapbook," I say finally.

"For me? About Skylab?"

I nod. "Because of the birthday thing. He thought ..."

"What?"

"He thought it would be fun."

"And now it's coming back."

There's something new in his voice, something odd. My gaze drops to the desk drawer. "Is there any more?"

When he says no, I'm relieved. Then I feel guilty for feeling relieved. Wouldn't it be better for Newt to have more of Dad, not less?

There's no way to know what's going on inside his head. There never has been. But whatever he's doing, I need to let him have this.

I shake up the can of spray and aim it into the corner.

I can't do anything about his Newtish thoughts but I can at least keep him safe from spiders.

Seventeen

For the next few days I watch three things: the sky, Newt and the news.

The first one makes no sense. I know that. It's not like anything's going to land on my head and if it was, I wouldn't be able to stop it, not even with an officially approved cardboard helmet.

Maybe it doesn't make sense to watch Newt either. He's going to do what he's going to do, no matter what anyone else says. He always has. And whatever he's doing with Skylab, it's probably safer than the Rudimentary Antenna Project turned out to be. If I'd known he was going to start climbing things, I'd never have given him that in the first place.

Still, I watch him. I watch him watching the news and there's a brightness to his face, a shine in his eyes that makes me feel uneasy. That makes me keep on watching.

All through the Skylab news, Newt scribbles in his notebook. He turns to us and repeats things Orange-Tie Man just said, as if we maybe weren't paying attention.

Did you know that Skylab is actually a laboratory. SkyLAB, get it?

It's logged about 2000 hours of experiments and taken over 170,000 photos.

Did you know that three manned missions have been made to Skylab?

It's like a house as well. It has three whole storeys. It has its own sleeping areas and a kitchen.

You can actually live there, Frankie. Did you know that?

Did you?

Mum sighs when the news is on but she doesn't turn it off. The whole world is watching now, so why shouldn't we? And it's not like it's forever. Once Skylab is down, we can get back to normal.

Whatever that is.

Whenever that is.

It's two weeks away and then it's three weeks away. It'll be here in seventeen days, or maybe ten. Sometime after July 7, probably. Sometime before July 20, most likely.

"Probably! Most likely!" Mum glares at Orange-Tie Man as if she holds him personally responsible. "Why can't you wait until you have some actual facts?"

Orange-Tie Man's gaze is steady. "We remind the public that there is no cause for alarm. The North American Air Defense Command is monitoring the situation closely from its subterranean headquarters."

Strangely, Mum doesn't find this reassuring. Neither do I. How come they get to be underground while the rest of us are stuck up here with our cardboard helmets and our church bells and things getting weirder every day?

All over the world, people have started to panic. They're ringing NASA up with crazy suggestions. On Monday we hear a bunch of them on the bus. Ronnie doesn't usually let us have the radio on in the morning because it's *Podge and Dazza coming at you with the Top 40* and he says it isn't even music and how come they never play something called Acca Dacca? But now, he turns it up loud and everyone goes quiet.

We should shoot a missile at Skylab! someone says.

We should fill a robot plane with dynamite and set it on a crash course!

We should send astronauts up to attach balloons so it will float into outer space!

When Newt hears that one, he laughs out loud.

When Kat hears that one, she says, "I volunteer Jeremy!"

When Jeremy hears what Kat says, he leans across the aisle and knuckles her in the shoulder.

"Don't forget your salad bowl!" I say, because I'm next to the window and I know he can't reach this far.

Podge and Dazza are laughing too. "Some creative ideas there!" Dazza says. "But I think it's a pretty safe bet that Skylab is still coming down."

"And that's good for you," Podge adds, "because if you can predict when, you could be a winner!"

One of the newspapers is running a competition, they say. You have to guess when Skylab will re-enter the atmosphere – to the day, the hour, the minute, maybe even the second if your psychic powers stretch that far. The person who gets the closest wins a pedometer, which is this new thing that counts the number of steps you take.

"Cool!" Jeremy says. All around us, kids start chattering, throwing out dates and numbers and theories.

"A what-ometer?" Kat frowns. "That's a weird idea. Why would anybody want to count their steps?"

I shrug. "Who knows?"

But then I think *hang on*, because I'm staring at Newt, in his usual seat down the front. And suddenly I wonder, suddenly I think I know. Newt would want to count his steps. He'd want to take little short ones and long, loping ones and see what difference it made. He'd want to fiddle with the buttons on a newfangled gadget. He'd want to open it up and see how it worked.

The walls of his room. All those maps and numbers and calculations. All his muttering about orbit paths and velocity and angle of re-entry and *working something out*.

It's perfectly and utterly Newtish, isn't it?

Maybe it's as simple as that.

When I ask him, he actually snorts.

"A what?"

We're walking up the hill after school. He's hurrying and I'm racing to keep up. For some reason I can't stop counting my steps.

"Pedometer. It was on the radio."

He's looking at me like this is the craziest idea he's ever heard.

"And in the newspaper. I thought ..." I veer to one side to avoid a patch of mud. Newt steps directly into the middle, covering his shoes in sludge. He stumbles a little, then rights himself, and looks back at me.

"I'm not entering a *competition*. That's not *science*. It's people guessing. Anyway, I ..."

"Anyway what?"

A faint smile plays on his lips. "Just wait. You'll see."

All right, I think as I jiggle the key and watch him disappear down the hall. As I empty his bag and scrape mud off his shoes. He's not worried about Skylab and he's not trying to win a pedometer. *I'll wait, then. I'll see.*

If Newt won't tell me what he's up to, what else can I do?

Besides, I've got better things to do than try to drag an answer out of him. I've got heaps of stuff to organise. Because Kat's coming. She really is. Mum got the new roster and we sat down on the weekend and looked through her diary forwards and backwards and then forwards again, until we finally found a date.

It's two weeks away, but that's okay. Because it's definite. Wednesday, July 11.

Even though it's still June, I flipped the wall calendar over to July. I circled July 11 in red texta and then I circled it again, just because. You can see the circle from the kitchen and the table and the couch. It stares you in the face when you walk in the front door.

There's no way anyone can possibly miss it. Which means it's really happening. Which is good. Which is great.

But which is also making me weirdly nervous. I can't remember the last time Kat was out here. It's always been easier for me to go there, with them being so close to town and her mum not working and everything. And now, when I think about Kat being here, the house feels different. Everything seems sort of cluttered and shabby compared to their place.

At first, I'm only going to clean my room. But

once that's done I start noticing other things – dust on the mantelpiece and the knick-knacks, cobwebs in the corners and behind the furniture, dirty marks on the kitchen cupboards.

I tell myself I'm being ridiculous, because it's not like Kat's going to notice that and even if she did, why would she even care and you can't fix everything even if once you get started it feels like you should.

Still, I move the couch a bit to cover the worn patches on the carpet. And then one of the chairs, to cover another patch.

And when Mum asks whether something's different about the lounge room, I shrug, as if I have no idea what she's talking about.

On Thursday I look for the air mattress. Kat's going to need that and I haven't seen it for ages. When I finally find it, stuffed inside a cupboard in the laundry, I think of spare sheets and a quilt and when I get those out, they smell like someone's grandma.

I'm hanging them on the line when Mum pulls up the driveway. She shakes her head as she gets out of the car. "It's not a visit from the Queen, love. It's just–"

"Hey, Frankie!" The front door bangs and Newt comes running out.

"Goodness!" Mum raises her eyebrows. "To what do we owe this pleasure?"

Lately, we hardly see Newt. He practically lives in his room, appearing only for dinner and the news, and after someone's banged on his door over and over to remind him he needs to have a shower sometime and maybe brush his teeth.

"Where's that story you used to read me?" He goes on as if Mum hasn't spoken. "The one about the bears."

It's so completely out of nowhere that I almost laugh. "*The Big Honey Hunt?* It'll be on the bookshelf in the hall. But what —"

"I looked there. Anyway it's not that one." He jiggles on the spot like a runner waiting to take his mark for a big race. "It was a couple of years ago. It was about some people who got turned into bears."

I frown. "I don't think so."

"I remember you reading it to me! It was like a folktale or something."

"Oh, right. Yeah, that was for school. The Greek myths."

We did them a couple of years ago with Mrs Mitchell. I don't remember much about the bear one but a lot of the stories were really cool. Kat and I did a project on Theseus and the Minotaur and made a maze inside a shoebox.

"So where is it?"

"It wasn't mine. It was from the library."

"Oh, okay. I'll get it tomorrow." He's halfway to the front door again already.

"Not the school library," I call. "Kat got it from the one in town."

There's silence and then he turns back, looking at Mum. "Can we go sometime? I really need it."

"I don't know, love." Mum grabs her bag and locks the car. "Things are pretty busy right now. We'll have to see."

Newt knows what that means. But he doesn't argue. He just stands there for a few seconds, then runs back inside.

Mum stares after him. "I wonder what that's about."

So do I.

Eighteen

On Friday afternoon Rachel is a bank teller. *Because I'm good at maths and I like working with people.*

It's almost shockingly normal. Mrs Easton looks so relieved I think she might weep. I glance at the clock. 2.55. There's still time for one more.

My eyes dart around the room, searching for inspiration.

Queen Elizabeth stares down from her painting. I wonder if she likes being the Queen. *Because you get to rule the Commonwealth*, I think, *and pay for lollies with your face.* Then I bite my lip so I won't laugh, so I won't draw attention to myself.

Mrs Easton's eyes rest on me for a second, then skim past to Dale.

"Round two," she says.

He's ready.

He strides to the front, wearing Jeremy's puffy jacket.

"What do you reckon?" I whisper to Kat. "Astronaut or FBI agent?"

She raises her eyebrows. "Maybe both?"

But the joke's on us, because Dale's going to be a zookeeper — *because it looks really cool and I like animals only not boring ones like vets do* — and the jacket is to keep him safe from lion attacks. Then Jeremy jumps up and says he would never have let him borrow it if he'd known it was going to be shredded by lions.

"Sit down," Mrs Easton says through gritted teeth. She looks like she's about to say something else, then sighs and picks up a pile of papers from her desk. "All right, one last thing before you go."

Kat sits up straight. "Finally!" she whispers.

It's our *Storm Boy* projects, coming back.

Mrs Easton places them facedown on people's desks. Sometimes she pauses to make a comment, something quick like, "Nice work" or "Watch your spelling" or "The word *ratbag* has no place in a book report".

When she gets to us, she stops. "Well done, girls," she says. "Excellent work."

Kat's poster is rolled up but anyone can see that it's covered in ticks.

When Mrs Easton sets mine down, she rests a hand

on my shoulder. It's only for a second but it's long enough. "Really outstanding," she says quietly. I don't think I've ever heard her say that before.

Kat unrolls her poster. There are big red ticks everywhere. Alongside *Habits and Habitat* there are two right next to each other.

"Wow," I say. "The rare double-tick."

Kat flips the poster over, then groans. "An A! So close. Maybe she really doesn't give A-pluses." Then she turns to me. "How did you go?"

I haven't checked yet. I'm not sure I want to. My project looks like nothing next to Kat's. It's just two sheets of plain foolscap stapled together, three of the four pages filled with tightly spaced writing.

Kat frowns. "Where are the ... oh!"

When I turn it over, there are ticks after nearly every line. Big and small. Double and ... triple?

And at the very top, my mark, underlined and circled in red.

A+.

"Wow," Kat breathes. "I don't believe it."

Neither do I.

Mrs Easton's written a comment on the last page. I can see the red pen through the paper. But I don't look now. I roll it up into a neat tube so it doesn't get creased, and when the bell goes I tuck it into the side pocket of my bag.

Kat is quiet as we walk to the bus, but while we sit waiting to leave, she turns to me. "Did Mrs Easton say you could do yours differently?"

"What do you mean?"

"It's ... you didn't have any headings or anything. And we were supposed to do Character and Setting and everything."

"I did all that," I say. "I just did it differently."

She reaches down towards my bag. "Can I have a look?"

"Oh, I–"

Before I can finish, Ronnie spins around. "Hey, is your brother coming or what?"

When I realise what he means, my stomach drops. Newt isn't here. Not in his seat. Not coming towards us across the playground.

I feel suddenly hot. Why didn't I notice? I should have noticed.

"Hang on," I say. "I'll ... hang on."

While Ronnie drums his fingers on the steering wheel, I run and check Newt's classroom. No sign of him or his bag.

I check the toilets and sick bay and then the library.

And that's when I work it out. Because Newt might not be there but Mrs Harris is. And she says he came in at lunchtime looking for a book on the Greek myths.

Which they didn't have – at least not that exact one. They had one a bit like it but he wasn't allowed to borrow it on account of *1001 Spectacular Science Facts for Junior Einsteins* being long overdue.

"*Unacceptably* overdue," Mrs Harris says. "Do you happen to know where–"

I don't hear the rest, because I'm already out the door, Newt's voice from last night echoing through my mind.

Can we go sometime? I really need it.

He wouldn't have, would he?

Yeah. Of course he has.

I clatter up the steps of the bus, stammering at Ronnie. "Sorry! I forgot we're not getting the bus today."

I'm sliding my bag out from under the seat when Kat grabs my arm. "What do you mean? You guys always get the bus."

"Not today. We're ... meeting Mum in town." I stumble down the aisle without looking back. Ronnie's already reaching for the lever that closes the door.

"Good thing someone remembered," he mutters.

Kat stares out the window as the bus pulls away but I don't meet her eyes. I loop both bag straps over my shoulders, my heart racing.

It's about twenty minutes to the library – if I walk. Maybe ten if I run.

I run.

My feet pound the footpath. My bag jolts on my back.

I'm bound to catch him on the way, I think. Newt isn't exactly the fastest runner.

One more block and then I'll walk a bit. That's what I tell myself at every corner. And then I get to the next one and keep running.

Why aren't I catching him?

What if I'm wrong?

What if he's back at school with his nose in a comic book, wondering where the bus went?

I keep running. One more block, past the milk bar and the newsagent and the laundromat. Then another one.

And finally I see him in the distance.

"Newt!"

I'm gaining on him faster than I expect, and a few seconds later I know why. He isn't running towards the library. He's running away from it, towards me.

"Frankie!" He's panting, red-faced, clutching a book to his chest.

I slow to a stop and wait, letting him come to me. When he does, it's all I can do not to shake him. "What are you doing?"

"Sorry! Is Ronnie angry? We'd better hurry."

He goes to take off again, but I grab him. "It's too late for the bus, Newt. It's gone."

His face falls. "Sorry," he says again. "I thought I'd make it back in time. It took ages to find the book."

It's worse than I thought. He didn't run off after school. He left class half an hour ago pretending to go to the toilet, and never went back.

"I had to," he says simply. "It was an emergency."

He's holding the book in front of him like a shield. There's a familiar picture on the cover — a man on a chariot being pulled by horses.

I feel a surge of irritation. "How can the Greek myths be an emergency? It's your own fault if you left your homework too late. You can't just—"

"Homework?" He gives me an odd look.

And all at once I know why. It was Year Four when we did the Greek myths. It's Year Four when everybody does the Greek myths. But Newt's in Year Three, which means he's not doing it for school, which means ...

I have absolutely no idea.

"Never mind." Suddenly all I feel is tired. Does it really matter why his Newtish brain told him he needed to *actually* have that *actual* story right now? Why a kid who's always said you should focus on one thing at a time is suddenly studying antennas and Skylab and UFOs and ... bears?

All that matters is that we're here, instead of where we should be.

"Wait." Newt's eyes widen. "How are we going to get home?"

"Oh, *now* you're thinking about that?"

"I was coming back!" he protests. "If the book had been in the right spot, I would've ..."

I don't wait to hear the rest. I just set off again — slowly, this time, because there's no hurry any more.

"Come on," I say. "This way."

Nineteen

At the hospital we sit in the waiting room on hard plastic chairs.

Newt reads his book and I watch the hand on the wall clock move slowly from one minute to the next.

3.40. 4.00. 4.20.

I wonder how long we should wait.

I know this is the way Mum comes out, but maybe I should've gone down to the nurses' station, got someone to let her know we're here.

I don't want to interrupt her while she's working but I don't want to sit here until five o'clock either. If she knows we're waiting, she might be able to finish earlier. Especially if I tell her about the chairs.

I wonder why they make them so uncomfortable. Maybe it's so you'll only wait if you're really sick. So you'll get up and leave if you possibly can.

I'd do that if I could. If there was any other way of getting home.

4.30.

Newt looks up from his book. He's got a frown on his face as if he's concentrating, trying to puzzle something out.

"Hey," he says. "You know how you said I could ask about Dad?"

It's so sudden, so out of nowhere. It takes me a moment to find my voice. "Yeah."

"I need to know what time they took off."

"What time they ..." I stiffen. "You mean Dad's plane?"

He nods.

"Why would you ...?" I trail off. Nothing in me wants to know the answer to that question.

"I told you. I'm working something out."

"I thought that was about Skylab."

"It is! It—"

In the quiet of the hospital, his voice is suddenly loud. I glance around, putting a finger to my lips. "I don't know what time they took off. And you don't need to either."

"I do. And you said I could ask about him."

"About *him*. Not about that." I try to make my voice

solid and steady, a thing that won't crack. I look anywhere but his face — at the floor, down the hall and finally up at the clock again.

4.31.

4.32.

It's long enough. I stand up. "Wait here."

"But—"

And then I walk away.

In the corridor my shoes squeak on the shiny floor. From the rooms on either side come the murmur of TV and low voices, and every now and then a long electronic beep. Most doors are closed but some sit open, the beds inside hidden behind curtains.

I haven't been here for ages but it's a small place and I know the way. At the end of this corridor there's a desk with a glass window where the nurses sit and do paperwork. Even if Mum isn't there, I can ask, get someone to find her.

Voices float around me. TV voices. Visitor voices.

Call now for a free measure and quote!

You're looking well, Meryl.

Kellogg's Cornflakes just seventy-nine cents a box!

What a sweet little thing! Eight pounds!

Only Milo has that unique chocolate flavour.

Oh, you'll bounce back before you know it.

Bounce back.

Is it the voice that stops me, or the words? Maybe both.

The door to the room is ajar. I can only see a sliver, but it's enough.

Mum's perched on the edge of a bed by the window. In front of her is one of those little tray tables on wheels. She's leaning on it, writing something on a pad of paper. Across from her, propped up on pillows, is a girl with a leg in plaster. An arm too. In her other hand, she's holding a plastic cup. She shakes it and scatters dice across the table.

"Four of a kind! Nice!" Mum scribbles on the notepad.

"Yeah, but only threes. You've got sixes two days in a row!"

"Well, you had a Yahtzee on Monday!"

"I think you've won again."

"Oops, sorry!" Mum's voice is light, teasing.

"Another game?"

Mum hesitates a moment, then reaches for the dice. "Just one then."

The clock on the wall above them says 4.36. The second hand ticks slowly, like it's moving through glue.

"Mum?"

Mum looks up and her eyes widen. "Frankie! What are you ... wait, where's Newt?"

"He's fine. He's in the waiting room."

"What—?"

"We missed the bus. So we came here."

It sounds so simple when you say it like that.

"Ronnie left without you? He can't—"

"It wasn't Ronnie," I say quickly. "It was our fault. It was ... we're fine. If you're still working, I can wait outside."

"No, no. I'm done for the day. We were just ..." She smiles at the girl. "We'll play another time, Louisa."

The girl nods. "It's not like I'm going anywhere."

Mum follows me out, pulling the door shut behind her. As we walk down the hall, I hear the rattle of dice in the cup. I love that sound. But I can't remember the last time we played Yahtzee with Mum. The last time we played anything.

In the car on the way home, Newt's glued to his book. Mum and I don't speak at first. She plays the radio until it cuts out.

Once it does, the silence is loud. It stretches.

Eventually, she breaks it.

"That girl ... poor thing. She's stuck there all by herself. Her mum works all the time."

So does mine.

"They're on a farm, about three hours out. It's really

161

hard for anyone to get in and visit." She sighs heavily. "You understand, don't you, love? There are just—"

"Yeah," I say quickly.

... *so many people that need helping.*

I don't know what I thought that meant. That Mum was wiping tears and emptying bedpans.

I know what I didn't think. That she was playing games with other kids while I save Newt from spiders and talk him off rooftops and make endless grilled cheese.

Mum twiddles the knob on the radio, even though she knows there's no signal around here. Then she turns to me. "You're a wonderful kid, love – the way you take everything in your stride. You miss the bus and you don't miss a beat. You walk right in and find me." She reaches over and squeezes my shoulder. "I'm so proud of you, the way you've turned out, the way you've ..."

I look over at her. "Bounced back?"

"That's exactly what I was thinking!" She laughs and ruffles my hair. "Maybe you're psychic or something!"

Newt glances up briefly. Our eyes meet in the rear-view mirror.

"Yeah." I resist the urge to lean forwards and fiddle pointlessly with the radio. "Maybe."

Things That Fall
From the Sky

The rattle of dice in a plastic cup.

Your mum playing a game with someone who isn't you.

You understand, don't you, love?

Your mum working late.

You understanding completely and then suddenly not at all.

Things that don't actually fall from the sky but feel like they do.

These things.

Twenty

Tennis balls. Super balls.

That's what I thought people were talking about, back then.

"They'll bounce back," they kept saying. "Don't worry."

Eventually, I realised they meant us. Me and Newt.

They'll bounce back. Kids always do.

And I couldn't shake the picture of us being whacked all over the place like we were in a game of bat tennis, ricocheting back and forth over the net until someone yelled *OUT!*

They'll turn out fine. You'll see.

When I heard that one, I knew they meant us. But what I imagined instead was Newt and me as biscuits, coming out of the oven on a tray.

Ooh! Look how they've turned out!

I heard so many things back then, when Dad was missing and our lounge room was full of people. I wasn't meant to, but I did anyway. With the hallway door cracked open, I could listen and still be out of sight. That way no one could ruffle my hair and tell me not to worry, in a voice stretched thin as wire.

I was six then. I didn't understand a lot of what I heard but there was one thing that came through clear as a bell. That it was important to bounce and turn out well. That it was important to be fine. And to make sure Newt was too.

So I tried really hard and the more I did, the more Mum smiled and said, "Oh, love. It's just so wonderful, the way you've bounced back."

That's how I knew what I was doing was right, and that I had to keep doing it.

* * *

"Oh, I know!" Mum says, as we twist spaghetti around our forks at dinner. "How about I do a roast when Kat comes over?"

"Yes!" Newt says. "With crunchy potatoes?"

"Of course! What's a roast without crunchy potatoes?" Mum turns to me. "What do you think, Frankie … that'd be good, wouldn't it?"

My mouth waters just thinking about it, but I don't reply at first. I know this is her apology but I'm not sure I want it. Not if it's one night and then things go back to the way they were, the way they are.

"Crunchy-bums!" Newt singsongs. "They're the best!"

Mum laughs. "That's right! I'd forgotten you used to call them that."

Me too.

I twist spaghetti around and around ... and around some more.

"Yeah," I say finally. "That'd be good.

I'm already in bed when I remember my *Storm Boy* project. With all of Newt's drama, I haven't even looked at it.

I turn the lamp back on and go over to where my bag hangs on its hook by the door. I unzip the side pocket and take the roll of papers out. Then I lean my back against the wall and slide to the floor. For a moment I sit still, my legs crossed, the papers in my lap. I'm nervous again but I don't know why. I got an A+.

I can almost feel that light touch on my shoulder, Mrs Easton's voice saying *Outstanding*. I don't care about the mark. I want to see what she says. I want to know what she thinks.

I turn the page. She's only written a couple of lines.

I read them over and over.

Brave is what she thinks. *Brave and honest and real.*

This is a fine piece of writing, she says. *A fine piece of thinking.* And it's strange because *fine* is such a nothing word, usually.

I'm fine. It's fine. The weather is fine. They'll turn out fine, you'll see.

But here it feels like an everything word.

A noise nearby makes me start. Someone out in the hall? Newt, making another late-night trip to the Shack?

I open my door and flick on the hall light. There's no one. And then I hear the sound again, and I breathe out.

I was right but I was wrong too. It's Newt, but he's not going anywhere. He isn't even awake. He's making those snuffling little sleep noises he's made since he was a baby. Mum said he'd grow out of it, but he never has.

I open his door a crack, spilling soft light in from the hall. He's so small under the heavy quilt, his fair head on the pillow, the mad-professor fuzz of his hair. On the wall above his head, there's a map of the solar system. The nine planets in their endless rotations around the sun, the curving lines of their orbits.

As my eyes trace their paths a thought comes to me like a whisper.

That's what we're doing – me, Newt, Mum.

Those cakes I made for Newt's birthday. I didn't get

them right at first. I had to move a couple of lines because the cakes were touching. Mars and Venus. Neptune and Pluto.

The planets don't do that. They're near each other but they don't ever touch.

They follow their own paths, which never cross.

I'm not fine. We're not fine. We haven't been for a long time.

I think I've known this for a long time too. I just don't know what I can do about it.

That girl in the hospital had a broken bone. That's easy to see, to feel sorry for, to try to fix. But what if something's broken here too and you just can't see it?

I blink and turn around, leaning in towards the wall by the door.

There are more articles here now – not a lot but a couple.

There are the usual updates – *Between July 10 and 20! Between July 10 and 18!* – but I've already seen those on the news. And there are other sorts of predictions, full of excitement, about what Skylab's going to look like once it re-enters the atmosphere.

Skylab to Light up Sky!

Like fireworks, I think. Or a festival.

If it takes place at night, the re-entry could make a spectacular sight. It would be well worth staying up for.

Like a movie, maybe. Like the drive-in. BOOM! Skylab!

Pieces could sprinkle right across the sky.

Like icing sugar on cupcakes – so delicate and lovely.

I wonder if it'll be like any of those things. They can say whatever they want, but no one really knows what's coming. No one's ever seen anything like this before.

I turn to go and my toe catches on something. There's a pile of papers on the floor, a book sitting on top. It's the one Newt got from the library. I bend down and pick it up. There's a scrap of paper in the middle, bookmarking a page, and when I open it, there's the story Newt asked about, the one about the bears.

I sit down in the wedge of hall light by the door, and read. And as I do it comes back to me – the story of a girl named Callisto who was turned into a bear by an angry goddess.

I can almost hear my own voice reading this to Newt. I can't believe I'd forgotten it.

Even before I read the rest, I know what's coming. How later the girl-bear was shot with an arrow, and saved narrowly from death by being plucked into the heavens and set among the stars. According to the legend, that's how Ursa Major – the Great Bear constellation – was formed.

It's funny to think that people really believed this

once, that it wasn't just a story they told. We have science now, so we know better, but sometimes I wish I could believe in those stories too. There's something almost magical about them that makes the world feel bigger.

Newt snuffles in his sleep and I'm glad he doesn't know what I'm thinking. He'd call me ridiculous, or worse.

I put the paper back in place and am about to close the book when I realise something. This isn't a random scrap of paper. It's a newspaper article, snipped carefully from its page.

The Mystery of the Missing Plane.

It's that weird article again, the one I saw on Newt's wall that afternoon.

He's taken it down, slipped it into this book. But why? Even if he couldn't find a bookmark, there's plenty of scrap paper lying around.

I hold the page up to the light and start to read. I read the whole thing this time, and the further I go, the weirder it gets.

It turns out that the pilot who disappeared without a trace is actually safe and sound. At least according to some psychics in New Zealand who made contact with him during a seance. He told them he's living with beings from the Great Bear constellation and will return to Earth by the end of this year.

My first impulse is to laugh, but something stops me

— a strange feeling crawling under my skin.

I look from the article to the book to the crazy cop-show mess on the walls. Newt mutters in his sleep and his voice is in my head, asking if I know what time Dad's plane took off. And then I hear myself, shutting him down, telling him he doesn't need to know that.

I see myself walking away.

And he's got no one to talk to then, so all he can do is come back to his room where he's working stuff out — Skylab stuff and Dad stuff and mythical, magical stories about people being rescued by the gods at the last minute. Being safe and sound — not dead and gone forever but just somewhere else, in the heavens.

Oh. No.

It's like that moment in a jigsaw puzzle when a piece snaps into place and everything starts to make sense. The things that looked like nothing before are suddenly something, small parts of a greater whole.

This isn't sense, though. It's the opposite of sense.

The paper's in my hand and my hand is shaking.

The weird and wonderful news. Dad would have loved it. He would have roared with laughter, and I would have too.

But I'm not laughing now.

Things That Fall From the Sky

Nothing, if they get beamed up by a UFO.

No one, if the gods decide to save them in the nick of time.

If they are *absolutely fine*, living in the Great Bear constellation, in the stars.

Nothing and no one.

If if if ...

A plane goes up and Skylab goes over. A man disappears without a trace.

Until ...

If ...

You can actually live there, *Frankie. Did you know that?*

Did you?

A small boy's birthday present starts falling back to earth.

Oh, Newt.

You don't really believe it, do you?

Twenty-one

Of course he doesn't.

There's no way Newt could think that, not even for a second.

That Dad's up there somewhere, in the stars.

That when Skylab comes back ... what?

That he's coming back too?

Even inside my head, it sounds ridiculous. Newt is science. He's logic and reason.

He's *Did you know people used to believe thunder meant the gods were angry?*

And *Actually it's caused by the sudden expansion of air.*

There's some other way this makes sense. There has to be. I'm just not seeing it, that's all.

Maybe if I'd listened to him the other day. If I'd talked to him.

Maybe if I talk to him now.

I wait for my moment. I don't interrupt him in his room. I don't chase him up the driveway.

The right time will come, I tell myself.

A few days later, it does.

It's Tuesday night and Newt and I are having dinner in front of the news. Mum's doing a double shift, so it's just the two of us. As soon as Orange-Tie Man starts talking about Skylab, Newt abandons what's left of his baked beans and grabs his notebook.

Orange-Tie Man tells us NASA's predictions now have Skylab coming down between July 11 and 16. *Almost certainly*, he says, which is a definite improvement on *probably* and *maybe* and *most likely*. Which sounds like someone might possibly know what they're talking about.

Newt flips the notebook open and writes something down, then underlines it.

"Once more, we stress that the risk of being struck by debris is extremely small."

Newt nods, as if they're having a personal conversation. "Six hundred billion to one, actually."

"Nonetheless," Orange-Tie Man goes on, "those wishing to shelter are advised that even large pieces of debris should not penetrate more than one roof and a concrete ceiling."

Should not? Without meaning to, I look up. From the

floor in front of the TV, Newt does the same. "Did you know," he says, "that in 1954 a meteorite crashed right into someone's lounge room? A woman was asleep on her couch and it hit her on the leg."

I glance up at the ceiling again, trying to resist the sudden urge to leap off the couch.

"Ann Hodges," Newt says. "That was her name. They named the meteorite after her. She got a massive bruise the shape of a pineapple." He stares at his leg almost wistfully. I reckon he's the only person in history who wants to be hit by a space rock.

I blink. What if it's as simple as that? What if the bears and the UFO are pieces of a completely different puzzle and all Newt's trying to do is work out where Skylab's coming down so he can ...

Huh? I can't believe I'm hoping my little brother is trying to get hit by a giant chunk of satellite.

Somehow it seems better than the alternative.

Fruit-shaped bruises fade. Broken bones heal.

But waiting for someone to return from the stars ... that could break your heart, I reckon.

And I don't know how you fix something like that.

Orange-Tie Man's moved on to *World Oil Shortage! US Petrol Madness!* Newt closes his notebook and I know he's approximately ten seconds away from disappearing into his room again.

"Hey, Newt." I slide down onto the floor beside him. "You're not trying to get hit by Skylab, are you?"

Right away I know that's not it. I know this look on his face, when he's thinking some new idea through quickly. I can almost see him running numbers in his head.

"You couldn't," he says finally. "You'd have to make sure it hit something else first, something thick enough to slow it down and you'd have to know how big the piece was ... how heavy it was because otherwise the velocity would—"

"Newt." I pick at a loop of carpet fibre, teasing it out with my finger. "The other day, when you were asking about the plane ..."

"Oh, that." He hesitates. "Don't worry about it."

"No, listen. I'm sorry for walking off." I work another finger into the carpet loop, stretching it sideways. "If you want to talk about Dad, we can. Any time you want. Now."

He gets to his feet, his notebook to his chest. "It's okay. I worked it out myself."

"Worked what out?"

"Don't worry about it," he repeats. He doesn't meet my eyes as he turns and heads for the hall. "I've got stuff to do."

"Newt ..."

He's gone. And I'm stretching the loop so tight one

end pulls free of the carpet so it isn't a loop any more but a long, loose thread. And then I'm wondering whether I should tuck it back in or cut it off with scissors or will that maybe leave a bald patch and if it does could I cover that with a chair or would it look strange having a chair right in front of the TV?

I can't stop my thoughts running and running so I turn back to the screen because even though it's off it's something to stare at and in the very centre, the faintest pinprick of light lingers and I wonder if I sit here for long enough without blinking, I can catch the exact moment when it disappears for good.

No.

There are plates to clear away and benches to wipe and Mum's cheesy baked beans to slide under the grill, because she'll be home any minute now. Probably.

Sometimes when you're doing a puzzle, you put a piece in the wrong place. At first it seems like it fits, but eventually it throws the whole thing off and you have to pull it out and start again from where you went wrong.

This thing with Newt must be like that.

It has to be.

* ✴ *

Over the next few days things get weird with Skylab. Weird-*er*, I should say.

On the radio in the mornings Podge and Dazza laugh so hard they can hardly speak.

On Wednesday they say it's coming between July 9 and 16 and while some people are scoping out smugglers' caves, others are planning parties. In Missouri, members of the newly formed Skylab Watchers and Gourmet Diners Society are going to wear hard hats and gather outside for a feast.

On Thursday it's coming between July 10 and 15 and a hotel in North Carolina declares itself "an official Skylab crash zone". They're painting a target on the building and inviting everyone to join them for a poolside disco.

On Friday it's coming between July 11 and 14 but don't worry because you can buy special Skylab insurance. If you get hit you'll get a massive payout. Or maybe your relatives will, depending on how badly you get hurt.

If you want to get hit, you can buy a special T-shirt with a bullseye on it.

If you don't want to get hit, you can buy a can of Skylab repellent. Podge and Dazza don't go into detail but I suppose you wait for the sonic boom, count the nanoseconds, then spray it into the air around you.

"Hey," Jeremy says, "I wonder what would happen if you had a bullseye T-shirt *and* a can of repellent. Do you reckon Skylab would hover in the air above your head?"

Newt turns around. For a moment he looks thoughtful,

as if this is a serious scientific question, as if he's about to say something in reply.

Then he sees me watching and his gaze slides away.

At school Jeremy asks again if he can be on emergency bell duty, "since Merv doesn't seem to be taking this seriously".

"Kindly refer to my husband as Mr Easton," says Mrs Easton. "In any case, I don't think ringing the school bell will have the desired effect."

"Yeah." Karen nods. "Everyone will think it's recess and run outside. Great plan, salad-bowl boy. You should pitch that to NASA."

Jeremy frowns. "I'd ring it differently. I'd think of a special signal or something."

"It could be like Morse code!" Dale says excitedly. "Only we'd spell out 'SKYLAB IS COMING. PLEASE TAKE SHELTER'."

"And 'THIS IS NOT A DRILL'," Jeremy adds. "You have to say that too, so people know you're serious."

"You mean the people who can understand Morse code," Kat says. "Which is basically no one."

"That's their bad luck," Dale says. "If you don't know Morse code, you don't deserve to survive. My uncle reckons—"

"Do *you* know Morse code?" Karen cuts in. "Tap SOS on your desk — go on."

Dale hesitates.

"Ha! I guess you don't deserve to survive."

"I know it!" Trevor calls out. "Dad taught me when we started going out on the boat."

"Me too!" Darren stands up. "I've got my badge and everything. I go to Cubs!"

"It's dashes and then dots."

"No – the dots are first!"

All around the room, kids start rapping their knuckles on desks. Dale tries to copy them, banging his desk lid. It's like the world's worst percussion section.

That's when Mrs Easton gets that look on her face. It isn't even time yet – it's still before lunch – but I guess she's desperate. "Right!" she says. "That's quite enough." She's already standing up, scanning the room. And something in me just knows.

And nothing in me is ready.

"Frankie," she says. "Help me out."

She smiles and it's like that hand on my shoulder, light yet steady at the same time. And I want to be that girl, the one she suddenly seems sure of. The one who got an impossible A+ and it definitely wasn't a mistake.

I want to be that girl so I stand up and go to the front of the room and I think once I get there it'll be okay. Once I get there, I'll think of something.

Because I'm brave and honest.

Because I'm fine.

But all those faces are in front of me and the noise in my head is so loud. All those knuckles rapping, those desk lids banging. All of them wrong.

Dot-dot-dot. Dash-dash-dash. Dot-dot-dot.

That's how it really goes. You have to know that. You have to know how to call for help when you need it.

Thoughts swirl through my mind, impossible to hold onto.

I could be a nurse or a journalist or a teacher.

I could be a radio operator.

Because dot.

And because dash.

My knees feel wobbly and my head as well. Kat's mouthing something at me and I can't make it out.

I want to be that girl but I can't.

I wish there was an air-raid siren, a special bell.

THIS IS NOT A DRILL.

"I can't," I say finally. "I'm not ready."

Mrs Easton looks me right in the eye. I want her to put her hand on my shoulder but she doesn't. She looks at me steadily and finally she nods. "All right. Next time, then."

It's not a question.

Twenty-two

On Sunday Orange-Tie Man is excited.

Excited but deadly serious. Because Skylab is coming this week. Definitely and without question. Which is even more reliable than *almost certainly*.

On Monday he leans forwards, talking faster than usual. "NASA has confirmed," he says, "that Skylab will re-enter the atmosphere between 8.30 am Wednesday and 1.30 am Friday. Once again, they stress that there is no cause for alarm."

The picture fuzzes and Newt frowns. He bangs the TV, bringing it back into wobbly focus. And I wonder how many times you can warn people not to be alarmed before all they start hearing is the word *alarm* and everyone ends up panicked without quite knowing why. And then I wonder if NASA would ever actually say there *was* cause for alarm, and if so, at what point? How many nanoseconds' warning would we get, and would that even be enough to get the cap off the repellent?

"While the situation is still developing," Orange-Tie Man goes on, "new information just to hand suggests that Skylab's dying orbits will take it across Australia for periods of between a few seconds and eight minutes."

"Eight minutes!" A gasp escapes my lips before I can stop it.

That's a long time to look up and hope that a 77-tonne space station doesn't re-enter the atmosphere above your head.

Australia is a big place. I wonder if it'll go over us. I wonder if Newt knows.

When I turn towards him, I'm not sure whether I'm going to ask or not. I kind of want to know but I don't want to give him another reason to start talking, thinking, obsessing about Skylab any more than he already is.

I don't get to decide because before I can say anything, he lunges for his notebook.

"I knew it!" he says, and that strange brightness is there on his face again.

He shuffles forwards, as if he wants to get as close to the screen as possible, as close to Orange-Tie Man and what he's saying, what he's promising.

He scribbles in his notebook, so quickly I wonder how on Earth he's going to read any of it later, and that makes me think about the Earth, which makes me think about space and the stars and his Newtish ways and that he's only eight and how can I make sure he's safe and okay and fine and bouncing back unless I know what's going on?

The phone rings but I don't move.

Newt looks at me. "The phone's ringing."

His eyes are on mine. They're not on his notebook or the TV or staring at the wall of his room. It feels like he's actually right here with me for the first time in ages and like it's now or never, so I let the phone ring and ring until it stops and then I say it.

"Newt, you know Dad died, right?"

He freezes.

The phone rings again. He turns towards it.

I don't move. It'll be Mum, apologising for something. Asking about beans and spaghetti.

This is bigger. This is more important than beans and spaghetti, or even a roast with crunchy-bum potatoes.

The phone rings for longer this time. I wait. And wait. When it finally stops, I start speaking again.

"Just because they didn't find his ..." I can't say the word. *Body*. It makes him not-Dad, somehow. It makes him a thing. "Just because they never found him doesn't mean—"

184

"I know that." Newt jabs a finger at the button on the TV. "I'm not a little kid."

"Newt, listen ..." I begin, but then the phone rings again and he jumps up.

A few seconds later, the receiver clunks down onto the little table. "It's for you!" he calls from the hall. And by the time I pick the phone up, his door is closed and he's gone.

"What?" I don't mean to sound so annoyed, or maybe I do. Beans and spaghetti and grilled cheese and ...

"Sorry," Kat says. "Were you outside or something? Mum said to keep trying. She's freaking out about Wednesday."

For a second I can't think what she's talking about. It's like Newt has knocked everything else clean out of my head.

"About the sleepover? She wants to know what your ceiling's made of."

I sigh and then I tell her it's concrete. Definitely. Even though I have absolutely no idea.

Sometimes all people want to hear is that there's no cause for alarm. Sometimes telling them that is better than worrying about the truth.

* * *

On Tuesday Kat tells me it's okay. Her mum said she

can still come. And that's good, because on Wednesday, NASA is certain. More certain than they've ever been. Skylab will be down within twenty-four hours. Today, tonight, tomorrow.

We don't know this from the newspaper or the TV, but from the radio, which is giving hourly updates. The teachers listen at school, tuning in at recess and lunchtime, and possibly when they tell us they're ducking out for a second to grab something from the office.

Ronnie listens on the bus, hunched forwards over the steering wheel. After school he drives slowly on the way out of town and the whole bus is quiet. There's no one singing or yelling or throwing banana peel as a crackling voice says that down here on the south coast of nowhere, Western Australia, we are now *on the flight path considered most likely to see the death of the 77.5-tonne space station.* That if NASA's current predictions are right, Skylab's *charred remains* will start to *plummet Earthwards* just after midnight and that *parts of WA might be in the line of fire.*

They're saying "plummet" now, instead of "arrive" and "tumble". They're saying "line of fire" and "charred remains" instead of "sprinkle" and "spectacular".

And everyone is shocked and saying *What are the odds?* and *Do you reckon we'll see it?* and *Line of fire?* and *How can we find out what our ceiling's made of?*

Except for Newt, who doesn't seem surprised or

scared or anything like that. Who seems kind of excited and nervous but also weirdly calm.

And also except for me. Because I can't help feeling like I knew this was going to happen all along, and I'm trying to keep an eye on Newt without making it obvious because Kat's sitting next to me with her sleepover bag on her lap and the whole point of tonight is that it's not about him.

Before the radio cuts out, we hear one last thing:

With the situation changing hourly, space officials have stressed that they are guessing.

"Guessing!" someone mutters. "Thanks, NASA."

"It's not too late to buy a helmet!" Jeremy calls out. "I've got some in my bag."

When we get off, Newt runs ahead up the hill.

He doesn't have to wait for me to open the door today, because Mum will already be home. She even organised to finish early so she'd have plenty of time to spare. By the time we left school, she'd be peeling potatoes and basting the meat.

I have no idea what basting is but if it helps make the roast, I'm all for it.

Maybe it'll be in the oven already. I sniff the air, in case I can catch the smell drifting down. But there's only eucalyptus: that clean, fresh smell the bush gets after rain.

The roast wouldn't be in yet, I decide. She's probably

just got the oven preheating. She's probably …

When we reach the yard, my stomach drops. The carport's empty. Newt's jiggling impatiently on the doorstep.

Kat frowns. "Where's your mum?"

I get my key out, trying to act casual. "She won't be long."

Please let her not be long. Please let her not have forgotten. Please …

Inside, I glance at the oven. Maybe I should get it going, put the meat into the pan.

I flip the oven dial. How hot does it need to be? And how long does a roast take to cook? It's nearly four o'clock but it won't matter if we eat a bit late. Maybe I should leave it, wait for Mum.

I pour two glasses of milk and find some Scotch Finger biscuits in the back of the cupboard. I get the potbelly stove started then sit at the table with Kat, like this is what I do after school. I try not to look out the window. I try not to look at the clock. I try not to look twitchy while my thoughts race, while I wonder whether I should call the hospital, whether I should put the meat in the oven.

Kat glances down the hall. "Doesn't Newt want a biscuit?"

"He'll come if he does. Probably not, though. He's working on something."

"As usual." Kat dunks her biscuit. "What is it this time – homemade volcanoes or rudimentary antennas?"

She smiles and for a moment I want to tell her everything. About Newt's bedroom and the Greek myths and that weird newspaper article. I want her to laugh and tell me I'm being silly, what a ridiculous idea. As if he'd ever think that!

But it's our sleepover night and her voice is in my head. *I just wish it could be the two of us sometimes, you know? You and me.*

This is our night, our one night. And even if Newt does have some strange idea about Skylab, it'll be over soon. The Earth is more than seventy per cent water and *statistically speaking* Skylab will be down somewhere in the ocean, a thousand miles away. Eventually, Newt will pull the paper from his walls and put his notebook away and if he has a fruit-shaped bruise on his heart, I'll try to help him fix it.

Because I've turned out so well and that's just what I do.

Kat nods towards the window. "Imagine if Skylab came right over here. We'd have a pretty good view."

"Yeah." As I look out, I picture us sitting on the verandah while Skylab blazes overhead. Watching it like a movie playing on the dark screen of the night sky.

There are footsteps then, and Newt comes through

from the hall. I point at the table. "Want a biscuit?"

"No, thanks." He walks past into the lounge room then out the front door.

Everything in me wants to get up – to watch through the window and make sure he stays in the yard. But I make myself stay put. I dunk my biscuit and drink my milk through the crumbs that have gathered on the surface and whenever I feel myself starting to worry, I count crumbs instead.

Thirty-six, thirty-seven, thirty-eight …

"So," Kat says, "do you want to work on your thing for Friday?"

She offered to help again after last week and I said yes because what else was I going to say and obviously I need all the help that I can get. I wish I didn't, though. I wish I could just …

Stop looking out the window, Frankie. He's fine.

"Yeah," I say. "That'd be good."

Kat gets her pencil case and an exercise book from her bag. "I'll make a list. Then we can write pros and cons and—"

There's a noise outside, a thump on the roof. A bird, maybe. Or a possum. We get them in the roof sometimes, making a racket.

Kat frowns. "What was that?"

Before I can answer there's another sound, different

now. A series of small sounds — not at all like a possum that runs around madly not caring who hears it, but slow and deliberate and quiet, like something — someone — trying not to be noticed.

The sound of footsteps.

He's not a baby. You don't have to watch him every second.

But this is different.

He's eight, Frankie!

"He's only eight, Kat."

I don't mean to say it out loud. As I run for the door, I hear my voice like it's coming from someone else.

But there's no time to be surprised by it because then I hear something else.

"Frankie!"

It's too late to do anything — to yell *Newt!* or run to get the ladder, which maybe I shouldn't have hidden in the first place because at least that was safer than him doing what he's done.

Which is to climb the tree near my window, crawl along the wide branch and jump across the gap onto the roof.

Which was easier on the way up than it is on the way down.

It's too late even for me to stand underneath and have the wind knocked out of me.

It's too late to do anything but watch him fall.

Things That Fall
from the Sky

Newt.

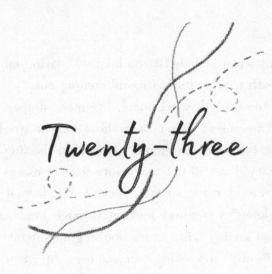

Twenty-three

By the time Mum gets home from the hospital, it's seven o'clock.

The second time she gets home, I mean. This time with Newt, who has his arm in a cast.

"Greenstick fracture," Mum said when she called earlier. "Could have been a lot worse."

The first time she got home was approximately 4.15. Approximately seventy-five minutes after she was meant to be home; approximately seventy-five seconds after Newt fell from the roof.

Just in time to pull up and wave and call out, "Sorry! I'm here! Sorry!", followed closely by, "Oh, my God! What happened?"

Luckily, Newt was sitting up by then so she at least knew he was okay. She at least didn't have a long, horrible moment when he was flat on his back staring up at her, his mouth moving but no sound coming out.

By the time they get home, I've made dinner. It isn't a roast because I didn't know how long it would take and also because even though I looked up "basting" in the dictionary, I'm still not really sure what it means.

Instead, I made apricot chicken. Kat helped too, if by "helping" you mean looking through cupboards for stuff and saying, "How come you've got so many cans of baked beans?" and asking over and over, "Are you *sure* it's okay to use the stove by yourself?" and "Do you think I should call my mum?" in case I didn't hear her the first few times.

When Mum's headlights sweep up the hill, I set the table and take the dish out of the warming oven.

Newt rushes straight to the TV. "I hope we haven't missed it!" He presses the button and a few seconds later the opening music for the seven o'clock news crackles into the lounge room. The picture is crystal clear.

Mum comes in shortly after. When she sees the table, she stops. "Oh." She holds up a newspaper-wrapped package. "I bought fish and chips."

"I cooked," I say. She could have told me.

"Why don't we save that for tomorrow, then?" As she sets the package down on the table, the smell of salt and vinegar makes my mouth water.

I shrug and ladle chicken into a bowl. "I don't feel like fish and chips."

In the end, we leave both on the table.

"People can choose what they want," Mum says. "If there's leftover chicken, we'll save it for later."

As soon as I taste it, I know there's going to be plenty of leftover chicken. Maybe it's because we didn't have any apricot nectar. Maybe it's because I'm not actually sure what nectar is in the first place. I thought it was something to do with bees or the gods. I ended up using apricot jam mixed with hot water, while Kat stared at me and said she was sure her mum wouldn't mind popping over to help.

Mum eats fish and chips. "They won't keep," she says. "No point wasting them."

Kat tries the chicken. A few minutes later, she pushes her plate to one side and reaches casually for a potato scallop, like she was planning to all along.

Newt fills his plate with chicken and takes it over to the TV.

"It's the last night!" he says. "We have to watch. Plus, look how clear it is!"

"Hardly worth a broken arm," Mum replies through gritted teeth.

From the grin on Newt's face I don't think he agrees.

Mum turns back to the table. "Apparently," she says,

"Newt went on the roof to adjust his antenna. Which — also apparently — he put up there weeks ago."

She's looking right at me. I chew my chicken slowly while Kat takes a handful of chips.

"I can't believe you let him on the roof, Frankie."

"I didn't *let* him. He just went up there."

"It was fuzzy yesterday," Newt says simply. "I fixed it."

"You're meant to be watching him! You know what he's like." Mum shakes her head. "You should at least have told me, so I could stop it happening again."

I almost laugh. You can't stop Newt doing things, not if he really wants to. All you can do is hide the ladder, hold your arms out, hope he doesn't hit the ground too hard.

Anyway, how would Mum have stopped him when she's not even here? All of a sudden I want to list all the things I haven't told her over the years. All the things she's never had to hear, never had to deal with.

But Kat's sitting across from me, staring. Tonight was meant to be about the two of us and somehow it's all about Newt again.

The TV gets louder and we turn towards it. Newt has his hand on the volume knob and his gaze fixed firmly on the screen. Which is full of Skylab.

Skylab will be down tonight, sometime before 7.49 tomorrow morning. This seems oddly specific and I wonder why they don't just say 7.50. Maybe they're trying to sound sciencey, like the Brookline Institute.

"There will be nine orbits between now and then," Orange-Tie Man says, "with two of those being directly over Australia – one at 11.09 pm and one at 12.36 am."

He holds up a card with a big map of Australia on it. There are two lines drawn across it as if it's wearing a sash. One goes across the east coast and the other goes right over here.

"State Emergency Services are on high alert," he says, "and a direct telephone link has been established between NASA and our official Skylab watchers in Canberra."

Newt glances out the window and as he does I see that flash again, of something on his face I can't quite read. Something sort of nervous and excited and thoughtful and worried, all rolled into one. He's tapping his foot, twitchy, the way he gets at the front door after school. As if he's waiting for someone to turn the key to a door he's desperate to go through.

At the very end of the bulletin, Orange-Tie Man gives us his most reassuring look, the one he usually saves for news about the nuclear arms race. "NASA advises," he says, "that on Skylab's final orbit around Earth, if there is any possibility of it falling on a populated area, they should be able to correct it at the last minute, sending it harmlessly into the ocean."

197

"See," Kat says, "I told you they wouldn't let anyone get hurt."

"They can't do that!" Newt says. "What if ..." He trails off, then turns to Mum. "I'm staying up. I have to—"

"No, you're not," Mum replies firmly. "It's a school night. And there's been plenty of drama for one day. I want you to have a shower and get ready for bed." She glances at the clock. "Have you set up the air mattress, Frankie?"

I haven't. I was going to do it before, after we'd played Yahtzee. Which we never got to do. All we got to do was cook and eat and get in trouble.

The batteries in the pump are dead so I blow the mattress up puff by puff, taking little breaks when I feel lightheaded. Kat offers to help but it's kind of gross asking a guest to swap spit with you so I keep going, pressing with my hand until things feel firm. That'll be plenty, I tell myself. That'll be enough.

By the time I've finished and the bed's made up and we've had our showers, it's 8.30. A game of Yahtzee only takes about half an hour but Mum says it isn't fair for us to stay up when she didn't let Newt.

"If you promise to keep your voices down, you can talk in bed for a while," she says. "How about that?"

Some sleepover, I think as I click the light off.

I should probably just be glad the sheets are clean.

Twenty-four

We're quiet at first, then after a while Kat rolls over. The mattress makes a squeaking noise as she turns towards me.

"Come to my place next time. It'll be easier."

I don't reply. I'm not pretending to be asleep or anything. I just don't know what to say. I know she's right but I don't want her to be.

"Even this weekend, if you want. Mum won't mind. Hey, maybe we could try for the drive-in again."

It's the way she says it, I think. How easy she makes it sound. Like all she has to do is ask and everything will fall into place.

Something about it makes me feel ... I don't even know what. It's like I'm stuck somewhere between sadness and anger. And maybe that's what makes me say what I do.

"I know your mum *won't mind*. I know that."

No sooner are the words out of my mouth than part of me wants to haul them back in.

But a bigger part of me doesn't.

Maybe it's the darkness. Funny how you can say things there you wouldn't say face to face. Funny how it opens you up.

"I know she'll meet us at the bus," I say, "and make biscuits and ..."

"Biscuits?" The mattress makes a squeaking noise. "What's wrong with biscuits? I *like* biscuits."

Her voice is lighthearted, like she thinks I'm making a joke. And why wouldn't she think that? Why wouldn't I be? It's not even Kat I'm angry at. It's Newt. It's Mum. Why couldn't he be normal for once? Why couldn't she be home on time?

The lamp clicks on. Kat's turned it on and she's smiling because it'll be *much easier* if we have a sleepover at her place. Because she can plan it out all perfectly and nothing will go wrong. No one will be late, or too tired, or *missing, presumed* ...

I reach over and turn it off again. It's my room. I get to decide.

"I don't want to go to your place," I say. "I mean, I do, but ..." I don't know how to say it. That this was meant to be *my* thing. Something I was doing, at my house, with my mum. "I know your mum can do it. I just ..."

I just want *my* mum for once. I want her here, with us – with me and with Newt and not spinning out there in the dark somewhere, in her steady, untouchable orbit.

I want, I want. I can't even say what I want. Maybe that's why I end up saying something completely different.

"We don't all get fancy bread rolls made for us, you know." The words spill out before I can stop them. It might not be Kat I'm angry at but she's the one who's here.

There's a sharp intake of breath. "What did you say?"

I want to explain, only I can't. I can't tell her Mum's never here, even when she is. It feels like it isn't my secret to tell. And I can't tell her about Newt – the way he twists me up with worry – because she already knows that and she's sick of it.

Neither of us has moved but the space between us feels further somehow, heavier.

"Nothing." There's a lump in my throat so hard I can't swallow. "Don't worry about it."

"It wasn't nothing," Kat says quietly. "I heard what you said."

The silence is thick with something. I'm glad I can't see her face, even gladder she can't see mine.

"I don't get it," she says finally. "I was only trying to help."

"I know that."

"I help you all the time, with lots of things. I lent you all those books and showed you my whole *Storm Boy* project. I got you that cardboard and you didn't use it. You got an A+ and then you wouldn't even show me. Plus, you never told me what you were doing. If I have a good idea, I always tell you."

Everything she's saying is true, but ...

"I didn't *know* it was a good idea," I say. "I thought it might be really weird."

"Then you got an A+."

"Yeah, but—"

"Forget about it." There's a brittle edge to her voice. "I'm going to sleep."

She flops back down on the mattress and rolls over, facing the door. Then a few seconds later, she starts speaking again. "I know you never asked about coming camping either, by the way."

"I did," I say. "I ..."

"No, you didn't. I heard Mum talking to your mum on the phone."

"I ... there wasn't any point. I knew I couldn't go. Mum needs me to keep an eye on Newt." I turn towards her in the dark. "You don't have any idea what it's like."

"Yeah, because you don't tell me."

"Because you don't want to hear. Because he's *eight*, remember?"

Even though we're talking quietly, this is definitely a fight. I've made it a fight.

Neither of us speaks. It's like we've both fired shots and now we're waiting to see what comes next.

And what comes next is nothing.

I pretend to be asleep until eventually I am. When I wake up groggily a couple of hours later, I wonder at first if the whole thing was a dream. Then I remember it wasn't, and instead wish it was, and wonder what I'm going to say in the morning.

The clock's red dots say 12.35. Kat groans in her sleep, shifting this way and that. I wonder if she's having a nightmare. Maybe she feels as bad as I do about what we said. Or maybe I've poisoned her with my chicken. I don't know which would be worse. At least if it's the chicken, she'll get over it quickly. I don't know what I'm going to do about the fight.

I know she's asleep but I reach down anyway. "Sorry," I whisper.

And then the loudest sound I've ever heard makes me jump out of my skin.

It's like the sky has split open. It's like we've been under a dome and someone's taken a giant hammer and cracked it right above our house. It's like thunder rolling on and on, only with the volume turned up so that it feels like it's inside your head and also all around.

In the middle of it I hear Kat's voice, half-awake, confused. "Frankie?"

It's as if a train is roaring through the house. The wind, the noise, the floor seeming to shake and every window rattling in its frame.

Outside the window it's light when it should be dark and then it's light again and dark, a hundred stars falling, or maybe a thousand.

And at first Dad's in my head saying, *You'll see one, short-for-nothing. Trust me on this.*

A hundred, though?

A thousand?

But these aren't like shooting stars — at least not the ones I've seen on TV. These are more like fireworks or little explosions ... or something I've never seen before, not even on a screen.

Over the hill behind the Shack, a bright orange ball is streaking across the sky, trailing sparks. And just as my sleep-blurred brain starts to focus — to know what this is because what else could it be? — I see the small shape running up the slope.

Oh no, oh no.

But also, *Of course.*

He was always going to stay up, no matter what anyone said.

"Frankie?" Kat says again, and she's definitely awake this time.

Only it's too late, now. It's too late to answer, because I'm already gone.

Things That Fall
From the Sky

Something.

A bright light.

A boom.

At the same time, only separate. Like lightning and thunder. Kids hiding under the covers. You see the flash, then wait for the rest.

It's okay, Dad always used to say. *It's nowhere near us. It's safe.*

But this? This is close.

How fast does light travel? And sound?

Well, actually ... Did you know that ...?

I'll ask Newt when I catch him.

If I catch him. If I can find him.

Out here in the bush – in the darkness, in the light.

Running and running and chasing.

Things that fall from the sky.

Skylab.

Twenty-five

In the distance, there are hundreds of fiery pieces.

Thousands?

Hundreds and thousands. I think of fairy bread, birthdays. Newt's very own space station.

Coming down now. Coming back.

Re-entering. Arriving. Tumbling.

Not sprinkling, but raining. Its broken pieces coming down hard and fast, like someone has shaken them up and hurled them from their fist.

The rattle of dice in a plastic cup.

White bursts of light that turn into red, like fireworks.

Spectacular! Well worth staying up for.

How far in the distance? How close?

Well, actually ...

I should be under cover right now. I should be in a

car or a house or an apartment. A school, even. I should be anywhere but here.

The chances of being hit are ...

What were they again?

Several huge chunks will fall to Earth ...

How many is "several"? How big is "huge"?

The only thing between me and the sky is bush. Leaves and branches.

And then not even that. When I reach the neighbours' paddock Newt's already on the other side, the circle of torchlight bobbing wildly. He's running faster than I ever knew he could. Over the fence as I watch, then out across the highway. The highway!

I breathe out. It's late. There's no traffic at this hour.

12.35 plus how much? The clock is far behind me. And Kat too.

I wonder if she's out of bed now. I wonder if everyone is. I wonder if Jeremy has his helmet on. I wonder if our ceiling is actually made of concrete.

I pick up my pace, trying to keep Newt in sight. There's no point calling. I know he won't stop.

Maybe it's the way he's running. That stumbling Storm Boy dash across the hills as if nothing can stop you, because it can't, because you're fixed on one thing only and it's the most important thing in the world.

Maybe it's because I always knew, in some deep part

of me. Because I was kidding myself thinking the puzzle added up to anything but this.

There's a burning smell in the air, almost electric. The bush is stirring around me – not just with night-time noises but others too. Birds have been dragged from sleep. They rustle and squawk, try their morning calls and then stop, confused. Dogs are barking somewhere, everywhere.

Newt crests a hill and I lose him briefly, then pick him up on the other side. We're heading towards the light, to where it was brightest. It's starting to fade now, becoming a dull glow on the horizon, somewhere beyond the next hill, and the next.

I have to catch him. Whatever this is, it's my fault. Mum's right – I haven't looked after Newt, not properly, not the way I should have. It's my fault he went to the Shack, that he found all that stuff. My fault he's out here in the middle of the night, running, wishing on his very own Newtish star.

I could have stopped this if I'd listened. If I hadn't shut Newt down when he asked about Dad, about the plane. If I hadn't turned away, said it didn't matter.

Exactly like Mum does.

The thought strikes me like a small blow. It didn't feel like that when I did it.

I can fix this, though. I have to. When I find him, I'll

listen to whatever he wants to talk about, whether I want to hear it or not.

I can't see where I'm going. I just have to trust my feet and the ground. Stones and fallen branches. Rabbit holes. Darkness.

At least Newt has a torch. At least he's prepared.

With a start, I remember his arm. I think of a bird dragging a broken wing.

It doesn't seem to be slowing him down. I stop thinking and just run.

* * *

It's four hills before I reach him.

Four stick-scraping, ankle-twisting, falling-over-and-getting-up-again, steeper-than-I-remembered hills.

I'm looking down, searching for his light. I'm panting, wondering where it's gone and how I'm going to follow without it, when I see him.

He's sitting on the ground a little way along. The torch is off and he has his back to me. He's tiny against the night sky, a small silhouette.

I don't know why he's stopped but I'm grateful for it. I bend over as a stitch slices my side. My heart is hammering in my chest like it's a wild thing, caged.

Twigs snap beneath my feet but Newt doesn't turn around.

I stand beside him, looking out across the trees and paddocks that stretch for miles.

Lights are coming on in houses. Headlights are nosing their way along roads. People are awake and wondering and coming out to see.

This thing that's happened, right on top of us.

I squat down, smooth away sticks and stones from the ground beneath me, then sit.

It's that loud kind of quiet again.

I wait.

"It broke up," he says finally. "It's all in pieces."

For a second there's something in his voice I've never heard before. Then he sucks in a deep breath. "I knew it would. It had to. Because of the atmosphere and the angle of re-entry and the velocity and ..."

It's like he's picking up speed with every word, talking himself out of something. Into something else.

He nods, as if he's listening to a conversation only he can hear. "Did you know that hundreds of pieces of Skylab might survive the re-entry process?"

"Yeah, I heard that."

"That's what I was doing," he says. "Looking for pieces. I—"

"Newt," I say softly. "It's all right. I know what you were doing."

He falls quiet, then looks up at me. Something

passes between us. The air is heavy with things I don't know how to say.

I'll never know how to say them, not properly. But do I need to? Do I need to snap my thoughts – my feelings – into tight little sections with perfect neat headings ... or can I just start talking, trust the words to come out?

"When I was little," I say. "When Dad died ..." I hear his little puff of breath, feel his body stiffen. "You know *Gilligan's Island*?"

He hesitates, then nods.

"I thought Dad was there. Somewhere like that, anyway."

I tell him – about spelling out HELP with stones, about waiting and waving and the pilot coming low to give Dad a thumbs up.

It's okay, mate. We've got you.

"I *knew* he was there," I say. "He had to be somewhere."

"Yeah." He's fighting to keep his voice steady, a tightrope walker wobbling one way and then the other. "How old were you?"

"Six," I say. "And then seven and eight and ... sometimes still now." I pick up a stick and trace a line in the dirt. "I don't really believe it any more, though. I just ..."

We're on the tightrope together. I lean into him,

press my shoulder against his. He's still for a moment and then it's like I feel something gather inside him.

"I knew it wasn't real," Newt says. "I knew he wasn't coming back. But I couldn't ... I had to come, just in case."

"I know."

"It was dumb." There's a break in his voice.

"No, it wasn't."

"It doesn't even make any sense. I knew that the whole time."

"Yeah." I nod slowly. I think about all those nights of trees and ladders and me on the ground with my arms out wide. I think about the Brookline Institute and twelve million people. Plus one, maybe. "But things don't always have to make sense, you know."

He turns towards me. He looks at me with the strangest expression, like with everything that's stuffed into that head of his, this is something that's never occurred to him.

And also like it's a relief.

He blinks and looks past me, at the spreading night sky.

"Did you know," he says, "that even if you wish for something really hard ... I mean really, *really* hard ... it still doesn't make any difference?"

He's crying now – quietly at first, then louder, as if it doesn't matter who hears.

He puts his head on my shoulder the way he used to when he was little. And I let him.

It's okay, Newt. I've got you.

"Yeah," I reply. "Actually, I did know that."

Twenty-six

After a while we get up and walk slowly down the hill. There's a road at the bottom that will take us to the highway. And on the highway, there's a steady stream of traffic now – cars and trucks and utes coming from town and from properties all around, all of them heading out towards where the light was brightest.

To where Skylab fell.

I take the torch on the way down and Newt holds onto me a bit – for balance, maybe. Or something else.

"My arm hurts," he says. "I didn't notice it before, but now ..."

I nod. "We'll walk along the highway. We'll face towards town and–"

There'll be someone we know, I think – someone who won't mind giving us a quick lift home. It's the middle of the night, after all, and we're two kids, one of whom has suddenly remembered his arm is broken.

We're almost at the highway, when Newt points, his eyes wide. "Is that ...?"

For a second I think I must be dreaming. That none of this is real – the night and Skylab and Newt and me up on the hill. Because it's our school bus, with Ronnie at the wheel, slowing for a second when he sees us as if he's going to stop and pick us up and take us ... where?

He doesn't stop. He shakes his head as if maybe he thinks he's dreaming too. Then he accelerates around the corner and out of sight.

That's when I see the car – our old purple Datsun – coming towards us. Slowing like the bus did, only not at all like that because instead of accelerating when she sees us, Mum pulls off into the gravel, yanking the wheel so suddenly I think she's going to skid, and then the door flying open almost before she's come to a stop. And Mum climbing – almost tumbling – out, a jacket thrown on over her pyjamas, a wild look on her face.

"Oh, thank God." Something in her sags. She takes a step back and slumps against the car, as if she needs something to hold her up.

I check both ways, then lead Newt across the road.

"Are you okay?" Mum looks at him anxiously. "You

can't go running off like that! What on Earth were you thinking?"

"He's fine," I say. "We're fine. He wanted to see Skylab. I went after him."

Mum looks from me to Newt and her face softens. "You kids. You're so—"

Suddenly I just can't. I can't listen to how wonderful and mature and good at bouncing we are. I can't tell Mum we're fine, go back to the way things were.

Brave, I think. *And honest.*

"No, we're not." I sit down right there in the gravel by the side of the road, as if I've suddenly run out of steam, out of everything. Maybe I have.

"We're not tennis balls," I say. "We're not biscuits."

"You what?" Mum's looking at me strangely and I can't blame her. When I don't reply, she runs a hand through her hair. "Look, we're all tired. Why don't we talk about this later?"

She gestures to the car but I stay put. Newt doesn't move either.

"It'll be easier in the morning."

Easier.

I think that's what does it.

I'm crying. It's just a little, at first, and then it's a lot. "I'm not fine. I don't bounce! I can't ..." I'm sobbing and I don't know where it's come from and

I know exactly where it's come from.

Mum's bending over alongside me. "Oh, love. What's all this?"

"You're never home," I say. "I have to do so much stuff and I don't mind ... only I do. I do if ..." Something rises in my throat and I gulp. "Do you always have to work so much? It's like you put everything away and there's nothing left of Dad and now you're putting us away too, because it's easier and I can't ... I need ..."

"Oh, Frankie. It's not like that. It—"

"Yes, it is. It is. That's how it feels and that means it is."

Newt isn't saying anything. He just sits down beside me and kind of leans in, the way I did to him up on the hill. And all of a sudden, I wonder if he's been feeling this too.

How would I know when he's never said anything?

How would Mum know when I've never said anything? When all I do is act fine and grill cheese and do the exact right jiggle in the lock?

I need I need I need ...

Things I hadn't even thought of until now.

Things that just come tumbling out.

"Dad was never gone," I murmur, almost to myself. "You never told me he was gone. He was on an island with driftwood and ..."

"He what? But he never—"

"I never said goodbye. I never said anything."

"Oh, love."

I feel like I'm breaking Mum but I have to keep going.

"Then it was too late. And now it's always too late and we're supposed to act like he was never here, like he was never even Dad."

Mum sits down beside me and puts her head in her hands. "I'm so sorry, Frankie. I know it's been hard on you but I didn't know ... I had no idea."

Now Mum is crying. Now we're two people sitting on the side of the highway crying in the middle of the night while cars whiz past following a dead space station.

And now we're two people hugging doing all those things and I'm crying so hard I wonder if I'll ever be able to stop but at the same time I feel better than I have in forever.

"My arm hurts," Newt says, to no one in particular. "It's broken, you know."

Mum actually laughs out loud. She pulls back so we can see each other's faces, and looks me right in the eye. "Okay," she says. "We'll be okay. I promise."

We get to our feet and brush ourselves off. I open the car door for Newt and wait as he climbs inside, then give him back the torch. Mum's standing behind me and when I turn she puts a hand on my shoulder.

"Precious," she says softly.

I don't know what she means 'so I just wait.

"That's what I was going to say before. You kids are so precious. I don't know what I'd do if anything happened to you. I ... oh, God."

It's like we both realise at the same time. I look into the car, at the empty seats. Mum looks at me and then all around us at the bush and the hills and the darkness.

And then we both say it together.

"Where's Kat?"

"I thought she was with you."

And right at that moment, a voice yells my name and I turn to see her stumbling down the hill towards us.

Twenty-seven

"Frankie, wait!" There's a panicked edge to Kat's voice, as if she thinks we're going to drive off without her.

I stare at her and all I can think is, *How come she's in her pyjamas?* But then I realise I'm in mine too, that my bare feet are sore and I'm actually freezing.

And while I'm thinking this, Kat falls. She trips on something and goes head over heels.

I run across the road. She's about a hundred metres up the hill, sprawled in the dirt, leaves and sticks in her hair.

"My leg hurts." She groans as I squat beside her and I think, *Oh, no.* One sleepover, two broken bones. But then she tests her weight on it and gets shakily to her feet. "I think it's okay." She nods, almost to herself, then looks up. "Why didn't you wait for me?"

She means back at the house, I realise. It feels like that was a hundred years ago.

"I didn't know you were awake," I say. "Not at first. Then I saw Newt and ..."

"I was awake for ages," Kat says. "All the air went out of the mattress. I was so tired and then I was maybe half-asleep and there was that sound, like the world was ending. It was Skylab, wasn't it? I can't believe it."

"Did you see it?"

"A bit. I was trying to catch up, but I kept losing you over the hills. Then I took a wrong turn and had to double back. It was so weird, like being in a movie. All those lights ... and that weird burning smell." She grimaces and leans back against a tree. "I can't believe it came right over here. It looked like the sky was exploding. Then when I saw you going ... that was so dangerous! You should have stayed inside, under concrete."

"I don't think our ceiling's actually concrete. Anyway ..." I hesitate, but only for a second. "I had to go. I had to follow Newt. I ... he's my brother."

"I know. I know, Frankie." Her eyes meet mine. "And I had to follow you, because ..." I see her trying to slow her breathing, so she can talk. "I'm sorry about before. About everything."

I can hear Mum and Newt coming up the hill behind us. There's no time to really talk.

But it's enough for now, that one word: *Everything*.

"Me too."

"You know ..." She smiles. "The whole time I was trying to catch you, I couldn't stop thinking: *I'm running wild in the bush! I'm running wild in the bush!*"

I laugh. "Oh, no. I hope your mum doesn't find out."

"Don't worry." She holds my gaze. "She won't."

"Kat?" Mum crunches up beside me. "Are you okay?"

"I just tripped on a rock. I'm fine."

"Thank goodness," Mum says. "What a night! Let's head back, then. I think we could all use some sleep."

I go to follow, then stop. Kat hasn't moved. She's staring at the ground. "This isn't a rock." She bends down and touches something. "It's warm," she says. "But what ...?"

Newt shines the torch, and we all stare.

The thing Kat tripped over isn't a rock or a branch. It's a thick piece of metal about the size of a small plate. It's a greyish-green colour, almost circular but twisted in places, wobbly-looking as if it's been ... melted?

Next to me, it's like Newt's stopped breathing.

Kat looks at him. "Is that ...?"

He nods. "It must be."

"Should I ... is it okay to pick it up?"

"I don't think it's dangerous."

She reaches for it gingerly as if it's something

unpredictable, something she can't quite trust. But it's only metal — metal that went to space and came back again, that fell to Earth right at our feet.

"Here." She doesn't even look at it properly. She doesn't turn it over in her hands and study it. She holds it out towards Newt.

His eyes widen. "Can I hold it?"

"You can have it."

"You mean to keep?"

"That's why you were out here, isn't it? That's what you were looking for?"

He hesitates.

"Go on. It's a donation — for science."

Newt takes it — slowly and carefully as if he can't quite believe it.

He isn't the only one.

Mum frowns. "Are you sure that's not some piece of old rubbish? I thought Skylab fell all the way over there." She points off into the distance.

"Actually," Newt says, "approximately five hundred pieces were estimated to fall over a footprint approximately 6400 kilometres long, remember?"

Mum shakes her head. "I actually don't remember all that, Newt. But luckily I don't need to, because I've got you."

We head back to the car, Newt clutching his little

piece of Skylab. He doesn't take his eyes off it, not even to look at the road. I stay close to him and when the school bus comes roaring back in the other direction, going faster than even Ronnie usually drives, I grab his hand extra tight, just to be sure.

Twenty-eight

In the morning, Mum takes us to school.

For no good reason, she says. Just because.

She says she will, and then she does.

Which is lucky in the end, because the school bus doesn't turn up.

We don't find this out until later, of course, when the other bus kids finally get to school.

"We waited for ages!" Jeremy says but no one cares because the only thing they're talking about is Skylab.

The whole world is talking about Skylab. And it feels like maybe the whole world is coming to the south coast of nowhere, Western Australia.

There are cars everywhere and people all over the place – booking up the hotels and stripping the supermarket shelves. Some are driving out of town trying to find pieces of Skylab. Others are staying in town trying to find people who don't mind having a microphone shoved in their face, who don't mind talking on camera about what it was like when a space station fell on top of us.

Literally on top of us. Some people even found pieces in their yards. Dale's uncle has a hole in his back shed.

It was pure luck no one got hit.

NASA is very sorry. At least they are when they realise there are actual people down here and not just kangaroos. At first, all they could say was, "We assume Skylab is on the planet Earth, somewhere", which is not really the level of detail you want from the world's top scientists.

Apparently, there was a lot of confusion because the phones weren't working properly. Even the Skylab watchers in Canberra announced that it had come down safely over the ocean. Mrs Easton said Merv had to ring them up and say, "Excuse me, but it's actually fallen on our heads!"

"Good old Merv!" Jeremy says, and Mrs Easton doesn't even correct him.

In the end, it turns out NASA did it on purpose. Not that they meant to hit us, exactly, but late last night when it looked like Skylab might land on North America, they decided to make it tumble, delaying its re-entry.

It made a clean arc across North America, swept south over the Atlantic and finally broke apart above the Indian Ocean.

Above us.

People are angry. There are protests in the streets and letters to the newspaper. Kat says her dad is ropeable and the council is going to send NASA a littering fine.

I wonder if they'll actually pay it?

Maybe they can ask Ronnie to cover it. Because apparently he's about to become very rich. A radio station in San Francisco is giving $10,000 if someone can get there within seventy-two hours with a real piece of Skylab. He hasn't made it there yet but he's well on the way. We're lucky he didn't drive the school bus all the way to Perth in his hurry.

· * * ·

At lunchtime on Friday Kat passes me a bulging brown bag.

"I couldn't fit it in my lunch box," she says.

"Don't tell me you found another piece?"

Everyone's looking for Skylab. The headlines today said *Treasure Hunt* and *Skylab Rains a Fortune in Debris*.

Kat laughs. "Open it."

I do, and then I laugh, even more loudly.

It's a bread roll, with a twisty bit on top. It's burned

on one side and the twisty part looks like a troll face. Or maybe a tumour.

She grins. "I made it for you."

"There's nothing inside it," I say. It's literally just a plain bread roll.

"Yeah, sorry. It was too hard to cut, even with the electric knife. Mum said I left them in too long." She shrugs. "I smeared some brown stuff on the side, the way you like it."

I turn it over. "What is it?"

"Gravy. We had a roast last night."

I roll my eyes. "Yeah, of course you did."

We both laugh then, together this time. Because we're okay. We hardly slept on Wednesday night. Thursday morning. Kat squeezed into the other end of my bed and we talked and talked. I showed her my *Storm Boy* project and I told her ... not everything, but most things. Everything that was mine to tell. And she told me about how her mum drives her mad sometimes with her endless baking and her after-school chats.

And I said, "Oh, you poor thing! How can I ease your suffering?" because I knew she wouldn't mind. Because we're not fighting, even though we were before. Even though maybe we will again. Maybe you have to sometimes if you want to stay friends.

Just before the bell goes, Mrs Easton looks right at me. And I look right back at her.

"Frankie," she says, but I'm already out of my seat.

I walk to the front. My back's to the class at first but then I turn.

I could be a teacher, I think. *I could be a nurse or a journalist or ...*

I take a deep breath.

"When I grow up," I say, "I'm going to be an astronomer."

Twenty-nine

I don't have a salad bowl.

I don't have a puffy jacket.

All I have is me – my shaking legs, my thumping heart.

I didn't write it down, didn't practise it.

I open my mouth and trust the words to come out.

"Because I've always wanted to," I say. "And because my dad was one."

And although it's last thing Friday, the room falls quiet.

"It wasn't his job or anything. It was just his hobby. But he was serious about it. We had a Space Shack and a telescope, a really powerful one. You could see the surface of the moon right up close."

Without meaning to, I reach out my hand the way I used to, and every eye in the room follows.

"Because there's so much about space we don't know. That we won't know for ages. A long time ago people used to think the stars were gods, or that the gods were in the stars. Now we know that's not true but there's still so much to learn. And even though it's science it feels a bit like magic, as well. I like that about it, that it can sort of be both."

I don't know what to say next so I take a breath and look out the window. The school bus is pulling up. Mr Despotovski drove us this morning; I wonder if it'll be him this afternoon.

Yesterday, Mum came down and met us at the gate. *Just because*, she said. She's taking a bit of time off — not a lot, but a little. Enough.

Because there are so many people who need helping. Me and Newt. And Mum too. The three of us together.

I think we've talked more in the last two days than we did in the last year.

More about Dad than we did in the last six.

I showed Mum my *Storm Boy* project too. Kat said I should, and she was right.

It was more brave and honest than I could be face to face.

It felt like it would be strange to be there when she read it, so I left it on her pillow. Later that night she came in and hugged me, her cheeks wet with tears.

And I didn't pretend to be asleep, not even for a second.

"Frankie?" Mrs Easton says. "Are you finished?"

All at once I'm back in the room. "Sorry," I say. "I was thinking about the Milky Way."

The thing is, I've remembered something.

"My dad told me something a long time ago," I say, "and I'd forgotten it until now. I was only six when he died, so ..." I feel dizzy for a moment but I press my feet to the floor and keep standing. "Did you know that even though the planets have their own separate orbits, they can still affect other planets? They can draw them in closer. Or move them further away."

I look out at Kat and she's got the biggest smile on her face.

"Anyway," I say. "That's just one cool thing that we've learned about space. And that's all I wanted to say."

There's clapping and strange looks but mostly clapping.

"Well done," says Mrs Easton, and it's not "outstanding" but it'll do.

I head back to my desk, but before I sit down, I add one last thing.

"Oh, also. Space is amazing, and I really enjoy lettuce."

Thirty

It's cloudy tonight when we go up to the hill, the three of us.

The four of us, in a way. In every way that matters.

We don't have a shiny plaque but we have a "Welcome to the Universe" sign. I've written "Charlie Avery" on it and then "Dad".

And underneath that, "This is his place forever."

Because it is, right here. This is the exact and only place he belongs.

We don't have a marble stone but we have a piece of Skylab.

We have a photo too.

Mum said I could choose it and I didn't even have to think.

When I went to my room instead of the bookshelf,

she raised her eyebrows. When I came back with the photo, she smiled. It was a sad smile, and that's okay. It's actually perfect, because life is full of mess and mistakes and there's no point trying to hide it.

We're going to get the other photos out later. We're going to put them back inside their frames, set them up on the mantelpiece and the walls and any place we like.

That's for later. Now is this.

"Here?" Mum says.

I glance at Newt, then nod. It's a good spot – not in the Shack but near it. On top of the hill so it's close to the sky, and slightly to one side – the house side, so we can see it from the big window, so it's right here with us whenever we want.

Newt puts the Skylab piece down and I lean the sign against it. We dig them both into the dirt a little, fixing them in place. Then I pass the photo to Mum. "Here."

It's wrapped in plastic, sealed tight with sticky tape. But still it will weather. The wind, the sun, the rain. Eventually it will fade.

That's okay. Not everything lasts.

Mum tapes the photo to the end of the sign. And there we are – me on the couch, Newt falling, Mum lunging and Dad with his mouth open, roaring with laughter.

If you drew a speech bubble around the sign, he'd be saying "Welcome to the Universe!"

Mum sits back with a sigh. Then she looks up at the sky. "It's a shame it's so cloudy." She turns to me. "You still haven't seen a shooting star, have you?"

I shake my head.

"Did you know," Newt says, "that shooting stars are not actually stars but meteoroids?"

"I do," I say. "I did. I knew that once, back when ..."

He looks at me. "When what?"

"I'll tell you later," I say. "I'll tell you lots of things." I throw my arms up in a wide stretch. "Anyway, I saw Skylab, and that was like a thousand shooting stars."

"No, it wasn't," Newt says. "What it was like was lots of pieces of metal falling through the atmosphere."

I can't help myself, then. I turn and grab him in a big hug, pulling him towards me, and Mum too on the other side.

Newt wriggles his way clear. "What was that for?"

"Because you're an idiot. A perfectly Newtish idiot."

And also because he was right, in a way. Skylab did bring Dad back to us, just not in the way he was thinking.

I look up at the night and I'm glad of the clouds, somehow. There's something perfect about the way they blur across the sky.

You don't always have to see the stars. Sometimes it's enough to know that they're there.

A Note on History, Research and the Making Up of Stuff

While *Catch a Falling Star* is a work of fiction, it is inspired by an actual historical event and I have drawn closely upon this in the telling.

In July 1979, Skylab, one of the world's first space stations, fell out of orbit, showering debris across townships, farms and desert near the south-east coast of Western Australia. In the way of the times – that is, via television, newspaper and radio – this was a global media event. As the world waited, the months leading up to Skylab's re-entry were rife with speculation, wild predictions, outlandish proposals and absurd merchandising opportunities.

Catch a Falling Star is a fictional re-imagining of this time. In writing it, I made conscious choices about which elements to fictionalise and which to represent in historically accurate terms. While I have taken small liberties with news reporting — paraphrasing, splicing individual quotes together and so on — for the most part this material is quoted verbatim from primary and secondary sources.

All Skylab-related details — the timeline and technical details, the public and media response to its decaying orbit — have been reconstructed as faithfully as possible via newspapers and other historical records. Twelve million people really did try to levitate Skylab, others took out special insurance and cardboard Skylab Protection Helmets were an actual thing. (I am now the proud owner of one!)

The story of the missing pilot who was reported to be living in the Great Bear constellation is also true. The disappearance over Bass Strait in October 1978 of a man named Frederick Valentich remains a mystery to this day. For the purposes of the book, however, I altered one small detail. The claim by an Australian psychic that Valentich would return by December 1979 was made in August of that year. I wanted to use that titbit but my story finishes in mid-July, so I did what any opportunistic writer would do, and moved the date. In the book, Newt stumbles across the psychic's claim in June, enabling it to feed into his theory about his father and Skylab. I've made other small timing tweaks of this kind where I felt it reasonable to do so.

There are larger departures from fact too. I've ignored some events that took place during the period of the novel because they didn't serve my purposes; I've emphasised others because they did. I set my story in an unnamed, fictional town, loosely standing in for, but not actually representing, the West Australian town of Esperance, over which debris from Skylab ultimately fell. Likewise, none of the characters in the book are based on any real person, even where specific events in which they are involved reflect those that actually took place. For example, while there was in fact a young man who won $10,000 by hurrying to the USA with a piece of Skylab, he was most certainly not a bus driver named Revhead Ronnie.

I've taken creative licence. I've taken poetic licence. Let's face it: I've taken as many licences as I possibly could. What else would an opportunistic writer do? Skylab's fall to Earth was a fascinating event and I'm thrilled to have been able to find a way to share it with readers. I can only hope my little story is as compelling as the real thing was all those years ago.

Acknowledgements

The earliest seeds of this story were planted in my childhood when, at something like Frankie's age, I watched the news and the sky and wondered whether Skylab might fall in my very own backyard. But a seed is not an idea and an idea is not a story and a story is not a book. I have a head crammed full of childhood memories and that's where most of them will remain.

That this particular memory became a book is thanks to a comic-strip character named Linus van Pelt. There's a *Peanuts* cartoon I love in which Linus sits with Charlie Brown, their backs to the reader, staring up at the night sky. Linus asks whether people are allowed to take fallen stars home in buckets, and when Charlie tells him stars are too big for that, he falls silent. The rest of the strip is wordless and static until the final frame, when Linus quietly discards a bucket, and my little heart breaks.

This poignant little comic strip somehow bumped up against my memories of Skylab. It gave me the character of Newt, and with him the heart of the story. So my first and biggest thanks is to Charles M Schulz, the creator of *Peanuts*, and to Linus, whose quiet voice has always spoken so loudly to me that he feels real.

I'm also indebted to Colin Thiele, whose book *Storm Boy*, which was very important to me as a child, crept into my thinking as I wrote, and from there into the cracks of the story.

Because this is a book based on a real event, I did a lot of research in the course of its writing. I spent countless hours scouring digital records on the aptly named Trove and countless more squinting at microfilm at the State Library of WA. Resources such as these are invaluable and I'm hugely grateful to archivists, to those who record and preserve our history so we can keep returning to the well. This also includes strangers on the internet – people who write blogs about old TV shows and their favourite childhood lollies, and put together listicles with titles such as "You know you're a child of the 70s if …". In the same spirit, I thank the hive mind of Twitter – for spirited debate over things like whether we used to say *kiosk* or *canteen* or *milk bar* or *deli*, to give just one example. I have no idea how anyone wrote historical fiction before the internet.

It wasn't all Sunny Boys and *Gilligan's Island*, though. I had science questions too. And not just any old science. Astronomy. Astrophysics. There was only one thing to do: ignore anything I didn't understand and write the story the way I wanted to, knowing I could bend the science to fit later.

Sadly, it turns out that's not how physics works. And that's why this is the part where I thank Dave Owen, aka "Space Dave", at Te Awamutu Space Centre, and Matt Woods on behalf of Perth Observatory, who answered my questions speedily and expertly without laughing at me once.

This is probably the point where I'm supposed to say that any errors that remain are my own. But I worked very hard on this book so I would like instead to lay the blame for any mistakes, inconsistencies, typos or plot holes at the feet of Mrs Eunice Golightly, who is distressingly prone to sloppiness and inattention.

Almost finally, huge thanks to Walker Books Australia, who waited and waited and waited for this book while life intervened in more ways than I could ever have imagined possible. Thank you for your extreme patience, for the care you take with my work, for your faith that I would eventually deliver. I'd like to say I'll never put you through that again, but who would I be kidding?

Absolutely finally and endlessly forever — the biggest thanks of all to my glorious and irreplaceable editor, Sue Whiting, to whom I've already said all the things and I know she is totally against repetition and overly long sentences so I'll just stop now before I say glorious and irreplaceable again and she comes along to smite me with her glorious, irreplaceable and overly long stick.

About the Author

Meg McKinlay is the author of eighteen books ranging from picture books and young adult fiction through to poetry for adults. Her work includes the much-loved *No Bears, Once Upon A Small Rhinoceros* and the critically acclaimed *A Single Stone*, which won the 2016 Prime Minister's Literary Award, among other prizes. Raised in central Victoria, in a TV- and car-free household, Meg was a bookish kid, in love with words and excited by dictionaries. A former academic at the University of Western Australia, where she taught Japanese, Literature and Creative Writing, Meg is now a full-time writer and lives near the ocean in Fremantle, where she is always busy cooking up more books. **www.megmckinlay.com**

MORE FROM MEG McKINLAY

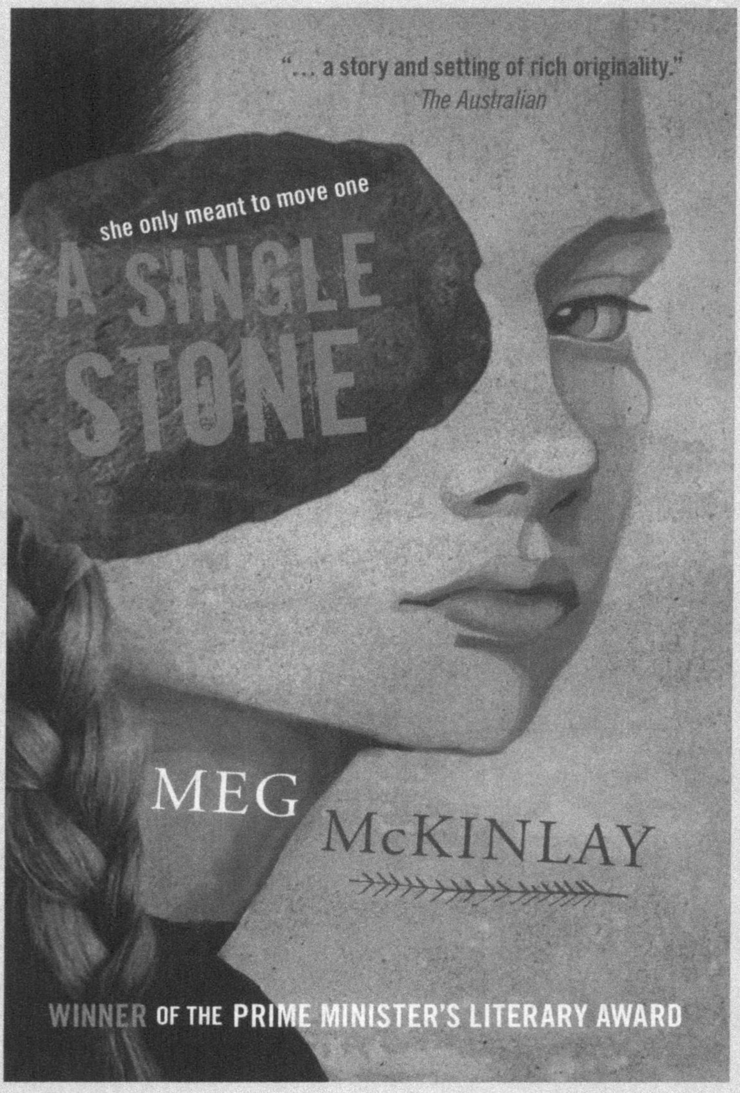

Every girl dreams of being part of the line – the chosen seven who tunnel deep into the mountain to find the harvest. No work is more important. Jena is the leader of the line – strong, respected, reliable. And – as all girls must be – she is small; her years of training have seen to that. It is not always easy but it is the way of the things. And so a girl must wrap her limbs, lie still, deny herself a second bowl of stew. Or a first. But what happens when one tiny discovery makes Jena question everything she has ever known? What happens when moving a single stone changes everything?

Winner, Prime Minister's Literary Awards, Young Adult Fiction category, 2016

Winner, Queensland Literary Awards, Griffith University Children's Book Award, 2015

Winner, Aurealis Awards, Best Children's Fiction category, 2015

Honour Book, Children's Book Council of Australia Book of the Year Awards, Older Readers Category, 2016

Short-listed, NSW Premier's Literary Awards, Patricia Wrightson Prize for Children's Literature, 2016

Short-listed, Victorian Premier's Literary Awards, Writing for Young Adults category, 2016

Short-listed, Adelaide Festival Awards for Literature, Young Adult Fiction Award, 2016

Short-listed, West Australian Young Readers Book Awards, Younger Readers category, 2016

Short-listed, West Australian Premier's Book Awards, Children's Books category, 2016

Long-listed, Davitt Awards for Best Crime Books, 2016

Annabel,
Again

MEG McKINLAY

Award-winning author of *A Single Stone*

Livvy and Annabel have been best friends forever. Together, they've survived kamikaze magpies, wacky mothers and a nemesis named Summer. Together, they've carried their netball team all the way to the finals. When Annabel moves away, Livvy is crushed. At her mum's insistence she embarks on a fast-track plan for moving on, for forgetting Annabel. Because what else can you do when someone's gone forever? And what can you do when, one year later, they come back? When they walk into class as if they were never even gone and sit down next to your nemesis? When it's Annabel, again, but nothing seems the same?

Short-listed, Western Australian Premier's Book Awards, Children's Books category, 2007

"Perfectly captures the nature of pre-teen friendships in all of their glory." Books+Publishing

Surface
Tension

On the day Cassie was born, they drowned her town. Twelve years later, she and her classmate Liam are drawn to the man-made lake and the mysteries it hides. As summer heats up and the lake waters become lower and lower, secrets are slowly uncovered. Can Cassie bring the shocking truth to light before it's too late?

Winner, Davitt Award, Children's and Young Adult Fiction category, 2012

Notable Book, Children's Book Council of Australia Book of the Year Awards, Younger Readers category, 2012

"Beautifully atmospheric ... A real page-turner."
The Sunday Age